⟨ AGƎNT ASHA ⟩

CHILDREN'S SPY AGENCY

QUESTION EVERYTHING

Agent Asha was made by many, many people coming together to create something we believe in. To our amazing team, publisher, family, friends, AACC community, thousands of special agents and every single person we've met along the way who has helped us on our journey – thank you.

This book is dedicated to you ★

First published 2020 by Walker Books Ltd
87 Vauxhall Walk, London SE11 5HJ

6 8 10 9 7 5

Copyright © 2020 Bright Little Labs
Illustrated by Anjan Sarkar
Photograph of Hedy Lamarr © SNAP/Shutterstock

With thanks to Anna Bowles and John Thorton,
and Sean Tracy, our tech consultant

The right of Sophie Deen to be identified as author of this work has been asserted by her in accordance with the Copyright, Designs and Patents Act 1988

This book has been typeset in Berkeley

Printed and bound by CPI Group (UK) Ltd, Croydon CR0 4YY

British Library Cataloguing in Publication Data:
a catalogue record for this book is available from the British Library

ISBN 978-1-4063-8272-3

www.walker.co.uk

MIX
Paper from
responsible sources
FSC® C020471

⟨ A G E N T   A S H A ⟩

 MISSION SHARK BYTES

SOPHIE DEEN

ILLUSTRATED BY
ANJAN SARKAR

WALKER
BOOKS

Prologue

A mole's bottom is a dark place to be. A duck's bottom is a wet one, and a hippo's bottom is a dangerous one.

The sea's bottom is all three, and that's exactly where the diver was swimming.

Kim Lau was currently about a mile away from the shore. According to her depth gauge, she was also 36 metres below the surface of the water. Each kick of her powerful legs was taking her deeper into the darkness and further away from the support boat. Her helmet torch wasn't lighting up much, except for a few startled fish.

She was looking for a cable on the seabed, but it was hard to see anything in the murky water. It still amazed her to think that lengths of glass and plastic at the bottom of the sea carried the Internet for thousands of miles, from continent to continent.

At least, that was what was supposed to happen. Three of the UK's most important Internet cables had been damaged in the last 24 hours. Kim worked for a cable-laying company, and her bosses had sent her team to inspect the cables and find out what was going on.

She scanned the seabed with her torch, ignoring the cold seeping into her diving suit. There it was! The cable was half-hidden among seaweed and sand, stretching away into the darkness. She swam closer.

The neat black casing had been ripped open and fibre-optic wires were spilling out. This wasn't normal wear and tear. This was serious damage. Kim reached for her camera to take a photo.

Wait… What was that?

User: Kim Lau
SCANNING…
3 short-fin squid
4 Atlantic cod
16 fart bubbles
1 DANGER INCOMING
Depth:
36 metres
1 undersea Internet cable
TAT 14
Optical fibre
Insulating sheath
Steel wire
Copper tubing
Plastic casing

Had something moved in the darkness?

Kim slowly moved her torch from side to side, her stomach lurching. She could hear nothing but the sound of her own breathing through her oxygen mask.

Stop being silly, she told herself. *You're imagining things*.

Then her torch caught the flicker of a dark shape circling the cable.

It was every diver's worst nightmare, swimming silently towards her. One sharp fin. One pointy nose. One gigantic, gaping mouth.

One hundred and one razor-sharp teeth…

Chapter 1

-.-. .- -. / -.-- --- ..- / .-. . .- -.. / - ....

April 14 - 09:45

Asha pressed the equals button on her calculator seven, eight, nine, possibly ten times. She could never resist messing around with a button, or, for that matter, a do-not-enter sign, a locked door or suspiciously loose floorboards. The closer she got to finishing an invention, the twitchier her fingers became.

"It's not working!" Asha scrolled through the code on her tablet and squished her nose in frustration. "There must be a bug."

"OMG! A bug! Where? Get it away from me!"

Tumble, a small hamster-like toy with bright orange fur, jumped up on Asha's bed.

"Tumble, relax! It's not a creepy-crawly bug!" Asha replied.

Tumble was small but loud. Asha had invented him when she was six years old, using a Poopless Pet™ toy, a motherboard from an old games console and a teddy bear. He had a tiny display on his chest that showed his battery level and a few basic emojis.

"Get the bug away from me, Asha!" Tumble shrieked, still hopping from paw to paw.

"Seriously! RE–LAX. It's only a computer bug in my code." Asha was looking at her tablet, searching for the problem.

Drone whizzed over and hovered above Tumble's head. "Let Asha concentrate on her coding, Tumble.

You're being a pest."

Drone was a nannybot and she'd been with Asha since she was in nappies. The metallic grey robot had logged every time Asha had cried, dribbled or farted. Now Asha was older, Drone was supposed to make sure she did her homework on time, brushed her teeth twice a day and never broke the rules.

What Asha's parents didn't know was that Asha had been hacking Drone for years. Mostly it had been to get around annoying parental controls, but also to help Asha get out of trouble, which for one reason or another, she never seemed to be too far away from.

"It's just this algorithm…" Asha mumbled. She was trying to invent a way to message her friends using two calculators. Asha knew that teachers loved calculators, so they'd never suspect her if she was playing with one in class. They'd just think she was doing maths.

"Algorithm. Totally. Got it!" said Tumble, scrunching up the right side of his face and winking at Asha.

"You remember algorithms, don't you? Like … the jam sandwich algorithm?" Asha asked, putting down her tablet. He still looked blank. Tumble's RAM was quite small.

"Please, you two, no more jam in Asha's

bedroom. It's a hygiene risk!" Drone cut in, but she was too late.

Asha slipped out of her bedroom and checked that no one was in the hallway. She then crept into the empty kitchen and found a tub of butter, a jar of jam, a loaf of sliced bread, a knife and a plate.

Back in her bedroom, she stood opposite Tumble. "Look at these things, Tumble, and pretend I'm a computer. That means I can't think for myself. I can only follow your commands." Asha lined up all the items on her desk. "I want you to give me step-by-step instructions, in the right order, for me to make a jam sandwich."

"No problemo," said Tumble. "First, you put the bread on the plate. Easy!"

Asha repeated his command in her best computer voice: "PUT BREAD ON PLATE!" Then, with stiff, robot-like movements, she picked up the loaf of bread and put the entire thing, wrapped in plastic, on the plate.

Tumble's eyebrows wrinkled. "No, come on Asha! Not all of it."

"NOT *ALL* OF IT," Asha repeated, starting to enjoy being a computer. "WHAT IS IT? WHAT IS ALL? ERROR. DO NOT COMPUTE."

Tumble paused before speaking again. "Gotcha… Open the wrapper. Take a slice of bread from the loaf. Then put the slice on the plate."

"OPEN THE WRAPPER. TAKE A SLICE OF BREAD. PUT SLICE ON PLATE." Asha followed Tumble's instructions to the letter.

"Then get some butter."

"GET SOME BUTTER." Asha smiled then sunk all her fingers into the tub and scooped out a huge, greasy glob of butter with her hand.

Tumble's mouth flopped open for a second, then he started laughing so hard that he fell on his back, his little paws waving in the air. "LOL, Asha! I didn't mean ALL of the butter and you need to use the knife, not your fingers!"

"Exactly!" Asha wiped the butter off her hands and onto her jeans. "Computers don't know what we mean unless we're super clear. You have to write a set of instructions in the right order to get a computer to do anything. That's the algorithm. And if the algorithm is wrong, you get a bug. And I've got a really annoying bug right now."

"Another bug? OMG! WHERE?" Tumble shouted at the floor. "Drone, do something!"

Asha rolled her eyes at Drone and tried not to laugh. She went back to her tablet. She pressed the equals sign again and finally a sharp beep sounded on Asha's second calculator. "HELLO ASHA" scrolled across the screen.

"Wow! The chatulator actually works!" Asha bounced up from her desk. "Demola is going to love this!"

Drone bobbed in the air in front of Asha, rotors whirring. "But you should pay attention during class, Asha."

Asha's hacks and upgrades hadn't managed to stop Drone's main function: worrying. Drone worried about the temperature ("Will you be warm enough, Asha?"), jumping down the stairs ("You might sprain your ankle, Asha!"), and even the toilet ("You should immediately empty your bowels, Asha!").

"I'd never use the chatulator when I'm learning

something. Only during assemblies. And breaks. And toilet breaks. And lunch. And maybe detentions." Asha said the last part under her breath.

Tumble jumped up from the desk, his tiny phone held out in front of him. "What's up, friendos! It's 10:06 a.m. and I'm chilling with the squad here at Tumble HQ. Big Saturday shout out to new follower @Sophie_Deen_ASC. Follow me living my best life for more quality content. #TimeForT! PEACE!"

According to Tumble's FaceSpace profile, he was the funniest, shiniest, smartest electronic hamster in Wembley and he liked to remind his followers at every opportunity.

Drone was unimpressed. "How many followers have you got now? Three?"

"Even Shelly B started somewhere, Smellycopter," Tumble replied, sticking his plastic tongue out. He was obsessed with Shelly Belly, the social-media celebrity turned tech-entrepreneur. Shelly Inc apps and games were the most downloaded of all time. Whenever a photo of Shelly's pet monkey-panda hybrid, Amanda, was uploaded to FaceSpace, the Internet almost crashed. "And I think you'll find I have way more than three followers."

"Probability suggests they are all bots." Drone whirled her propellers. "In fact, I'll scan for fake accounts now. Commencing scan..." Drone paused. "Scan could not be completed due to a connection error."

"You were saying?" said Tumble smugly. Asha's eyebrows pulled together. "Connection error, that's weird. I'll take a look at the router after breakfast. Not having the Internet will ruin the weekend!"

Chapter 2

. ---- -.-. . .-.. .-.. . -.- - / -.-- --- ... / .... ..
--. ... .-. . -.. / .. - / --- ... -

10:15

In the kitchen Asha was immediately hit by a wall of words.

"Good morning!" cried Dad. "Just in time for breakfast! The most important meal of the day! Especially for you, my wonderful pumpkin, and your BIG GROWING BRAIN!" He rubbed Asha's head, messing up her hair, and then tried to make her dance along to the song on the radio.

Asha studied his face. Dad was smiling and wearing his favourite King Jalebi apron, but he looked tired.

"Hello, Rani!" said Mum, looking up from the

spreadsheets on her tablet. Both she and Dad worked hard on their side business, Joshi's Jalebis. Judging by the piles of ghee, maida flour and sugar lined up on the side, they had a long day of cooking ahead.

"Morning, Mum!" Asha replied, sitting down at the table. Mum had called her Rani – her princess – for as long as Asha could remember. She was

more into prototyping than princesses, but she loved her nickname all the same.

The song on the radio finished playing and the news came on. "The country of Iceland has lost access to the Internet. Reports suggest that undersea cables may have been—"

Dad switched it off. "That's enough of you, Mr News Man. Breakfast time is family time! We don't want to listen to your boring blah blah blah!"

Actually Asha *did* want to listen. She had so many questions. How could an entire country lose access to the Internet? Why was Iceland called Iceland? Who was the first person to make ice cubes?

"Wait, Dad! How can the whole of Iceland's Internet be broken? And what have cables got to do with anything?"

"My genius pumpkin, you know more about this than I do!"

Asha sighed. She should have known better. Her Dad thought the Cloud was an actual cloud.

"Rani, you know enough about electricity to know that the Internet has to be carried by something. I can't see the cable that makes this light turn on, but that doesn't mean that cable doesn't exist." Mum pointed to the light in the ceiling. She was a whizz at DIY and she knew about how to think through a problem. "Now, tell me, what are you going to do today while we cook, Rani? Invent the next FaceSpace?"

Before Asha could reply, footsteps stomped down the hallway and Asha's older sister, Anushka, appeared in the doorway. She was wearing a baggy black T-shirt, ripped skinny jeans and a scowl. Anushka had been fun until a year ago. Now, she was only interested in music. Last week, she had recorded the neighbour's cat and mixed it with the sound of a construction site.

"Hey," muttered Anushka as she sat down.

"Hey," Asha responded distractedly. She really wanted to find out more about Iceland's Internet.

"Putie, turn the radio on." Asha activated the family's virtual assistant.

"Iceland's schools, hospitals and airports are all—" said the reporter.

"Putie, play Nush's playlist!" interrupted Anushka.

A horrible screeching filled the air.

"Putie, turn the radio on," Asha repeated, covering her ears.

"Putie, activate parental controls. Don't play anything!" At Mum's command, silence filled the kitchen.

"Much better," said Dad.

The family tucked into their masala eggs. Asha thought about how she could record her parents' voices and then code a program to bypass Putie's parental controls. She'd already created a VoiceFaker Program for Drone, so it shouldn't be too difficult.

"Asha, eat your breakfast before it gets cold," said Mum.

"Dis is del hmff," Asha said, digging in. Then she remembered not to talk with her mouth full. "Sorry." She tried again. "This is delicious."

"You're very welcome, pumpkin," said Dad. "Now, what homework do you have this weekend? I want you to finish that before you do any more tinkering with your gadgets." Dad poked at his tablet on the table. "And I think there was a message for you..."

Asha's parents had access to Anushka's and Asha's email and FaceSpace accounts. In theory, they could check everything that Asha sent or received, but they didn't know about her other three secret accounts. Neither did Anushka. Asha leaned over to see what Dad was talking about.

"The local library is opening a new shelf," he said, opening an email.

"Wow," said Anushka. "How very-not-exciting!"

For once Asha agreed with her sister. "That's cool, Dad. I bet they have more … erm … paper now." Asha tried to sound interested. "Let me see."

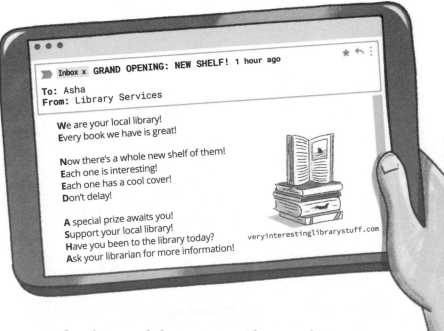

Inbox x **GRAND OPENING: NEW SHELF!** 1 hour ago

To: Asha
From: Library Services

We are your local library!
Every book we have is great!

Now there's a whole new shelf of them!
Each one is interesting!
Each one has a cool cover!
Don't delay!

A special prize awaits you!
Support your local library!
Have you been to the library today?
Ask your librarian for more information!

veryinterestinglibrarystuff.com

Asha skimmed the message, then read it again more slowly.

"Dad," she said thoughtfully, "does this message seem … weird to you?"

Dad nodded wisely. "Ah, that's how you write when you're advertising something. You use lots of exclamation marks."

There were certainly lots of exclamation marks on the Joshi's Jalebis website. But Asha was still suspicious. Something about it just felt … odd.

Asha played around with the words in her head. First she tried them backwards:

Ew era ruoy lacol yrarbil.

Then she tried missing out every other word:

We your library. Book have great. There's whole shelf.

Maybe not.

What about taking the first letter of every word?

Wayll…

That wasn't right either.

Suddenly Asha found what she was looking for. It was a code. Not the code that she used to write computer programs. It was an old-fashioned human code, where the words contained a hidden message. Once Asha saw it, it was obvious. The first letter of each sentence seemed to jump off the screen and dance around, while the rest of the email faded into the background.

The code said: **WE NEED ASHA**.

Chapter 3

.-- . -- . -- -... . .-.. / - --- / ---- ... . - ..

--- -. / . ...-. .--. - .... .. -. --.

10:29

Asha stuffed her eggs down as fast as possible,
almost choked, released a mini-fart, blamed
Anushka, and then ran to her room, shouting that
she was doing her homework.

"*Lookatthisemail!*" she said breathlessly, as she
forwarded it to Drone and scooted next to Tumble
on her bed. "The first letter of every sentence spells
out a secret message."

Drone scanned the email, her spam filter
beeping.

"Why does the library need you? You haven't

borrowed a book in one year, two months and seventeen days."

"I have NO idea," said Asha. "And why would they send me an email with a hidden code?"

"OMG! Maybe it's spies!" cried Tumble. "Or aliens. Or zombies!"

"Yeah, cool! Maybe you're right, and brain-eating zombies have taken over the library and instead of the police, they want us to save the day!" Asha was imagining the scene.

"Unlikely scenarios aside," Drone said, "it could just be spam. After all, 45 per cent of all emails are spam."

Asha stared at the posters on her bedroom wall, her thoughts racing. She had a weird, non-poo feeling in her stomach, like it was totally empty.

Perhaps the library wanted to encourage more kids to borrow books. Or perhaps it was a coincidence. Or maybe she had been selected by the government. The government owned the library, right? Maybe they needed her help to defeat a global group of… Asha was stuck. And why would they ask her, anyway? She'd never done anything *that* interesting before. Apart from that one time with Demola's balcony, the milkshake, the shoelace and the—

"This is highly unlikely to be a coincidence," Drone said, as though reading Asha's mind. "The library has never emailed you about a new shelf before, so it's unusual. But is it statistically unusual? It's difficult to know." Drone continued scanning the email suspiciously. "Did you see the link at the bottom of the message?"

In her excitement, Asha hadn't noticed the tiny URL. She clicked and waited for it to load. The Internet was definitely slow today. Eventually a website appeared on the screen.

Asha screwed up her face in disappointment.

https://www.veryinterestinglibrarystuff.com

WLLVC

Poetry Potatoes · *Rhubarb Romance* · *Spinach Science* · *Join Us!*

Taters, not haters!

Welcome to the West London Library Vegetable Club, which brings together people who are passionate about words and greens! We're a small and select bunch, always looking for new members.

Give peas a chance!

The West London Library Vegetable Club terms and conditions:

Members must carry an ID card which must include the member's name, age, favourite vegetable and a photo of a potato. Members can borrow three vegetables and three books per week. The vegetables are not to be eaten. If a vegetable is eaten, the member may have to pay a fine. Members will be punished for any late returns of vegetables. We do not like tomatoes and do not consider them to be a vegetable. All members must give peas a chance.

For full terms and conditions, **click here**.

Instead of finding a portal into a hidden world, she'd found a vegetable club! Maybe the email had been meant for her parents – they used loads of vegetables in their cooking.

"Oh," beeped Drone excitedly. "These terms and conditions are *very* interesting."

Asha and Tumble exchanged glances.

"My facial-recognition software tells me that you're not convinced," said Drone. "But I think you'll change your mind if you keep reading until Section 16, Clause 28."

"I'm just going to skip to that bit," said Asha, swiping up on her tablet.

"You'll miss the fifteen paragraphs about the dangers of paper cuts," warned Drone.

Asha wasn't listening. In among the tiny lines of type and long legal words, she'd found the clause Drone was talking about. At first, it looked like a normal piece of text. But Asha had learned to look for the tiniest of details when she was coding. She saw there was a hyperlink hidden in the last full stop of the paragraph. She clicked it.

After several seconds, another website loaded.

Whoa.

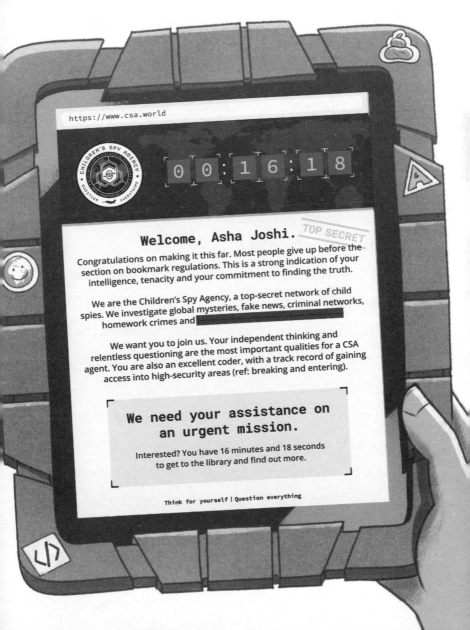

https://www.csa.world

00:16:18

Welcome, Asha Joshi. ~~TOP SECRET~~

Congratulations on making it this far. Most people give up before the section on bookmark regulations. This is a strong indication of your intelligence, tenacity and your commitment to finding the truth.

We are the Children's Spy Agency, a top-secret network of child spies. We investigate global mysteries, fake news, criminal networks, homework crimes and █████████████

We want you to join us. Your independent thinking and relentless questioning are the most important qualities for a CSA agent. You are also an excellent coder, with a track record of gaining access into high-security areas (ref: breaking and entering).

> ## We need your assistance on an urgent mission.
>
> Interested? You have 16 minutes and 18 seconds to get to the library and find out more.

Think for yourself | Question everything

"Spies," yelled Tumble. "I knew it!"

"You also said that it could be aliens or zombies," Drone huffed, annoyed at being outwitted by a robot-hamster with only 15 terabytes of RAM.

Asha wasn't listening.

Someone wanted her help on an urgent mission? She couldn't believe it. Maybe it was Demola playing a prank on her? Then again, could he really build a double-fake website? Unlikely. He didn't know a lot about HTML or CSS or any kind of programming language.

But Asha knew lots about coding. She was also pretty good at breaking into networks. Maybe the Children's Spy Agency really existed and needed her help. But … who were they? And why was there a time limit?

THE TIME LIMIT! Asha snapped back to her senses. She only had 16 minutes left to get to the library.

"We've got to run!" she said, leaping to her feet and panic-dropping things from her desk inside her backpack: her tablet, some raisins, a notebook, a torch, a banana, a couple of USB keys, a hairband and her lucky keyring. "Let's go!"

"Absolutely not," replied Drone, her pixels glowing red. "We can't just rush off because of a strange message from an unknown person. It is very dangerous."

Asha snorted. "The only danger at the library is that I might get a paper cut." She paused. Actually, she had no idea who had sent the email. Sure, Drone could be a bit overcautious ... but this time,

maybe she had a point. There was no way that she was going to admit this though.

"We'll be fine," said Asha, as confidently as she could. "I'll tell Mum and Dad where I'm going. You and Tumble are coming with me AND it's a library. Nothing ever happens in a library!"

Drone's turbines zoomed, creating a small gust of wind. "You obviously haven't read—"

Asha interrupted her. "Drone, help me calculate the most efficient route from here to the library. We have zero time to waste, so we should look for the quiet crossings. And …" Asha hesitated, "we should avoid the corner shop too. Otherwise, we'll just get distracted."

Drone's wings whirred. She loved a good route. "I am calculating the fastest route based on your instructions. Asha, if we leave now we can get there within the time limit."

"What are we waiting for?" Asha grabbed her backpack. "Drone, Tumble, let's go! Chalo!"

She raced down the hallway and poked her head back into the kitchen. "I'm off to the library to do research for my homework project about … circus life!"

"Rani, you have a project? You didn't tell me about it." Mum looked up from her chopping board. "Nush, can you go with your sister, please?"

"No!" Asha and Nush yelled at exactly the same time.

"I've got Drone with me, Mum, and I'll be back in half an hour. I'm meeting Demola there too. It's a really important project, and it's Saturday morning! That's the safest time ever." Asha was already out of her front door, Tumble and Drone in front of her.

"Rani, wait there! You can go, but I'm activating Drone's parental controls!"

"Away From Home controls activated!" said Drone in a soft lullaby voice. "Logging commencing."

"And you need to be back for lunch!" said Mum.

Asha sprinted down the street before anyone could say anything else.

Chapter 4

.- -. ... / - --- / - .... .. -. --- / .... --- ... /
-.-- --- ... .-. ... . .-.. ....

10:49

Asha arrived at the library with less than a minute to spare. She was panting heavily.

"I'm here!" she yelled, pushing through the big double doors. "Stop the clock!"

"SSSH!" An angry hiss came from a stony-faced librarian. Old women glared at her from behind their newspapers, and a father and toddler pulled a face over in the picture book section.

Asha's cheeks burned. Suddenly she felt silly. What had she been expecting? Secret agents with headsets waiting for her behind the bookshelves?

A hidden bunker in the library? Whatever she had been imagining, it wasn't anything quite so … library-ish. There were no agents, no investigations, no urgent missions. Not so much as a psst.

"PSST!"

Asha turned around to see a different librarian holding her finger to her lips. This one was friendlier and judging by her earrings, she loved otters.

"Tech section," whispered the librarian. "Third stack, top shelf. Take this and find the book that matches." She placed a card with a shiny holographic logo in Asha's hand. "You've now got … 43 seconds."

Asha did her best to run without looking like she was running, which was about as easy as reading with your eyes closed. She found the right block of shelves and peered at the books, looking for a clue.

Tumble hopped out of her pocket and scrambled up the shelves. He had stopped at an old and dusty book. "Asha, this book has a shiny thing on it like that card!"

"Yeah! Good spot, Tumble!" she whispered. She touched her card to the spine of the book.

The wall of shelves silently slid back, revealing the opening to a narrow shiny steel-lined tunnel. Before Drone could warn her about safety, Asha dived into the darkness and began crawling on her hands and knees. This was more like it!

She could hear the patter of Tumble's paws and Drone whirring behind her, muttering about all the dangerous things that could happen in tunnels. Her heart beat a little faster.

The passage led into a dark room filled with floor-to-ceiling screens. Asha climbed to her feet and the door to the tunnel slid shut, sealing off her exit. As she stepped forwards the floor underneath her lit up, scanning her

height, shoe size and eye colour.

Asha stood completely still. Where was she? And how was she going to get out? This room didn't look anything like a library.

The far wall was covered with holographic maps. There were blinking dots in faraway places like California, Nairobi and Stockport. On a stack of metal shelves, all kinds of gadgets were laid out in neat rows. Asha was about to take a closer look, when a glowing hologram appeared out of nowhere in front of her.

"Welcome to your local branch of the Children's Spy Agency, Asha Joshi," said the hologram. It was shaped like an enormous plate of masala eggs on toast, jiggling eggily on the spot. "Applause and praise on arriving here within the time limit.

You have passed the navigation and agility tests."

"Um ... what is going on?" asked Asha, wondering what agility was.

"I am named Hedy, and I am the central Artificial Intelligence Unit of the CSA." The computerized voice was coming from unseen speakers. "I have scanned your breath and determined that you ate masala eggs on toast for breakfast. Therefore, based on my data about human behaviour, I am  appearing as an object that you are familiar with, so you will feel more at ease. I have tried to mimic the exact recipe of your breakfast eggs."

"Wow," said Asha. "That's so cool. And gross."

"Do not eat the hologram," continued the voice.

"Um, yeah I won't,

don't worry," said Asha. "But who – or what – is the CSA?"

"The Children's Spy Agency, or CSA, is a secret intelligence network. We have agents all over the world and we only recruit the most extraordinary Homo sapiens. According to our reports, you have what it takes to join us. We have been monitoring you for some time, using information on your hamster's FaceSpace page."

Drone whirred at Tumble, who stepped forward waving a paw. "So great to meet a follower IRL!"

Hedy ignored him. "Our analysis shows that you ask 'Why?' on average 32 times a day, Asha Joshi. This is an advanced level of questioning which scores very highly, even among our top agents. We were also very impressed by the solar panels that you installed on the roof of your school."

Asha beamed. Her SolarSchool experiment had led to a new backup energy source, and she'd managed to give Demola some power to kick-start his Lunchtime Toastie Takeaway empire.

"And the way you upgraded your school's

cybersecurity after your teacher's email account was hacked was outstanding," continued Hedy.

Asha's grin grew even wider. She decided not to mention that it had been her who'd hacked the emails in the first place. To be fair, she hadn't told anyone about Mrs Penny's subscription to *Fart Control Magazine* ... yet.

"Our motto is: Think for yourself. Question everything. You are the ideal candidate for the Children's Spy Agency. When the world's governments have a crisis that their adult security services cannot solve, they turn to the CSA. We need you, Asha. Between 193 and 195 countries need you."

Drone flew towards the holographic plate of eggs and addressed Hedy directly. "As Asha's designated risk assessor, I have questions about your proposal. First of all—"

Tumble jumped in front of Drone. "Who are you? And why do you need me?"

Drone glared at him. "Why do you need *Asha*?"

The hologram flickered. "She is very good at

breaking into high-security computer systems. We need her help to save the Internet."

"Save the Internet?" Asha gasped. "From what? Viruses? Hackers? Parents?"

The image on the screen changed and Asha jumped back. Instead of masala eggs, Hedy had turned into a giant set of jaws.

The speakers boomed: "SHARKS!"

Chapter 5

-.. --- / -. --- - / ..-. . .-.. -..- / --- -. / - .... .
/ .. -. - . .-. -. . - -

10:58

"Sharks?" said Asha, trying to keep the quiver out
of her voice. "You don't mean actual sharks, right?
Are they a new hacking group, or something? Or
is it an acronym for … the Seriously Hardcore
Anarchist Rebel Kids?" Asha hoped so. Those
SHARKs sounded cool.

"Negative," said the holographic jaws. "Sharks
are large fish, commonly found in oceans, horror
movies and some seafood restaurants. Their
scientific name is *Selachimorpha*, and they can
grow up to 50,000 teeth over the course of their

lifetime. Humans are very afraid of them, even though you're more likely to be injured by a vending machine than a shark."

"O...K..." said Asha. "But what do sharks have to do with the Internet?"

Hedy transformed into a tangle of wires, that moved as if they were lips. It was only slightly less scary than the jaws had been.

"The Internet is a huge network of connected computers across the world. Information can be sent from one computer to another in the network," said Hedy. "The computers in the network are connected to each other via cables. Some of the cables run for thousands of miles under the sea."

"Cool! I had no idea," said Asha.

"Over the last 24 hours, there have been serious global issues with Internet connectivity. I'll now play a report from an engineer who went down to investigate a cable on the seabed."

The screen in front of Asha burst into life. A woman wearing a wetsuit was holding a diving helmet with a shaking hand. "This is Kim Lau reporting on Cable 97A. Conditions were as expected. I located the cable and looked for damage. I found a big tear right through it. The wires were completely exposed. I was going to take a photo, when I saw something moving in the darkness. It was a huge shark, swimming beside the cable."

The on-screen Kim swallowed hard.

"I swam away as fast as I could. The shark didn't follow, but stayed near the cable. But I wasn't taking any chances so I activated my panic sensor. I've never known sharks of that size in these waters before. Ever."

The screen flickered out. Silence filled the room.

Even Tumble stopped trying to press buttons.

"Whoa," said Asha eventually. "So the Internet is slow because sharks are attacking cables?" Asha wondered if she was missing something.

"We believe so," said Hedy. "Ten of the country's undersea cables have been destroyed. There are about 30 others. We are now at a dangerous point. If sharks attack any of the remaining cables, there will be a total collapse of the Internet here."

Asha's mind felt as tangled as the wires she was speaking to. An hour ago she'd been eating breakfast. Now, an AI hologram was telling her about secret agents and cable-munching sharks.

"Is that what happened to Iceland?" Asha said slowly, remembering what she'd heard on the radio.

"Affirmative," said Hedy. "We think the same pattern of attack will be used in countries all over the world."

"But WHY?"

"The Internet is essential to the daily life of 3.2 billion people, almost half of the world's population. Hospitals rely on the Internet, banks rely on the Internet and people need it to keep in touch with friends and family. Already today, Asha Joshi, you have used the Internet 33 times. At the moment, the Internet isn't owned or regulated by a single person. But if an individual was able to gain

control of it, they would become the richest and most powerful person on the planet."

Asha had never thought about the Internet like that before. But Hedy wasn't answering her question about sharks. "But why—"

Hedy cut across her. "The CSA fights injustice and abuse of power. We've received confidential information that the shark attacks are being organized by Shelly Belly, the trillionaire inventor of—"

"—LavNav and TWAG." Asha nodded excitedly, as she finished Hedy's sentence.

It wasn't just Tumble who was obsessed with Shelly Belly. Asha knew everything about her. At fourteen, Shelly had become the youngest person ever to win a Falcon Prize – the biggest prize in tech – for inventions like LavNav (an app for finding public toilets when you are out and about) and the TWAG series (Time Wasting Addictive Game). Now, at seventeen, she was the CEO of Shelly Inc, a global tech company that made search engines, apps, robots, toys, phones, smart houses, genetically modified pets, designer babies, antibiotics, hands-free poop-a-scoops … everything, really.

"Shelly Belly is very powerful. Her combined worth is more than the value of all of the world's pocket money and gold. The CSA has investigated

SUSPECT

PRIME SUSPECT: SHELLY BELLY

See Suspect File 42.7 - strong likelihood she's connected to the case.

SHELLY INC

ASHA'S MISSION

Infiltrate Shelly Belly HQ and secure the Operation Shark Bytes files. Test our hypothesis that sharks are eating the Internet cables. Is Shelly Belly behind the attacks? Find out how.

TOP SECRET

≡ Chattr

@realshellyb Today at 9.19 AM
Woke up to news of further loss of Internet worldwide. I'm so devastated. If you can read this, don't worry, my team and I are working on a solution</3#YouButBetter
Shared by 14k people ♥ 20.3k

@realshellyb Yesterday at 4.13 PM
Great meeting with @RicardoKonCarney just now while working my glutes on the elliptical #fitnessfriday. Expect some exciting developments from Shelly Inc soon!
Shared by 570k people ♥ 6.8k

@realshellyb Yesterday at 10.34 AM
It's a beautiful morning at Shelly HQ. My lovely team of dedicated employees are joking around as always. Look at this clown, lying on her face! I love my staff.

shellyinc.life
Shared by 38k people ♥ 58.2k

her in the past over the way she collects the personal data of her customers without consent, particularly data relating to the time they spend on the toilet. Now we believe Shelly is trying to cause a global Internet shutdown by using sharks to destroy undersea cables."

"How can she control sharks?" Asha asked, more confused than ever.

"We have inconclusive evidence. She might be luring the sharks to the cables. Or she might have trained a shark to attack the cables."

"But how will Shelly run Shelly Inc without the Internet? Surely she will be affected too?" Drone asked.

"Once news of the shark attacks become public, Shelly plans to replace the cables and launch her own Internet: ShellyNet. People will have to pay whatever Shelly wants to charge them, because there won't be any other option," said Hedy.

"So you think Shelly's doing all of this just to make more money?" Asha asked. "But she's mega rich already!"

"It is more complicated than that, Asha Joshi. Shelly and her corporation want complete control. If people are forced to use ShellyNet, all Internet-based services – email, instant messaging, video calling, banking, transport, music streaming, media streaming, social media, and yes, nannybots – will be under Shelly Inc's control. Shelly will be able to check your search history or your nannybot's log. If she decides that she doesn't want you to video call Nana-Ji or that a hospital can't have the Internet, she could block your Internet access."

Asha gulped. "That's really bad!" She reached for Drone.

"We predict that will only be the beginning. If users have to give their personal information to sign up, Shelly will know everything about everyone. She will own all your private data." Hedy flickered. "We fear this is just the first part of Shelly's plan. We strongly suspect she has an ultimate goal. Global mind control."

CASE BRIEFING:
THE INTERNET

Summary: Global connection

WARNING

Structure:

If the cables that connect countries to each other break, it's a problem. Whole countries could lose access to the Internet. We would not be able to send agents the same intel for missions. Other bad things would happen. This is dangerous.

Cable structure:

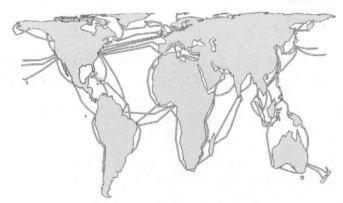

CSA BRIEFING: THE INTERNET

Importance:

  Location-dependent. In the UK, over 90% of homes use the Internet.

Used for:

 Systems   Banking

 Communications   Memes

 Shopping   Cat pictures

Risks:

⚠ Security breaches

⚠ People becoming idiots and forgetting to think for themselves

⚠ Robots taking over

Decoy opportunities:

Adults find the Internet very confusing. This can provide an opportunity for you to pretend to help while you break into systems.

NOTE: Our best agents know how to navigate using GPS or the stars. Do not overly rely on the Internet for anything.

Chapter 6

--· --- / -· --- - / ·- ··· --- / ·- -··· --- ··· - / ····

··· --- - --- -··· --- ···· / - ···· ·· ·-· - · · -·

11:04

Asha's head was spinning. It was a lot to take in on
a Saturday morning. She turned back to Hedy. "So,
Shelly is using sharks to attack the Internet. And
you need my help to stop her?" Asha was having
trouble believing that there hadn't been some sort
of mix up. Could there be another older, smarter
Asha Joshi out there, and the CSA email had been
sent to the wrong person by mistake? And was
Shelly Belly really behind Internet-destroying
sharks? Just last week, Asha had watched a video
of Shelly donating routers to schools.

"Affirmative," Hedy replied without hesitating. "We know there is a file called Operation DeepWater saved locally on Shelly's computer system. The file will tell us exactly how she has trained the sharks and which cables she is planning to attack next. We can use this information to stop the attacks and expose Shelly. It will not be easy to bring someone as powerful and in the public eye as Shelly Belly to justice. We need every piece of data in that file."

"Right," said Asha, her mind racing. "Shelly Inc will have state-of-the-art cybersecurity." Hacking a system like that was going to be a challenge, but a seriously fun one. Ideas immediately started bubbling out of her. "A cyberattack will raise so many alarm bells. Shelly will be on to us in no—"

Hedy interrupted her. "We do not want you to hack Shelly remotely. A hack will alert Shelly that her systems have been compromised. We require you to infiltrate her headquarters in person and gain access to the high-security ShellyServer console. The console is located in Shelly's office.

You will retrieve the file from the server, exit the building without attracting attention and upload the data to the CSA's network, as quickly as possible. Another agent will then pick up the mission."

"But why me?" Asha asked, wondering how she was meant to get inside Shelly Inc. "Why not use that agent?"

"We admire your bravery, Asha Joshi, and your ability to talk yourself out of a tight situation. We have chosen you because Mission Shark Bytes will be similar to the time when you climbed up the drainpipe to your headteacher's third-floor office and hacked her computer."

"Oh, erm, yeah … I needed to make sure that me and Demola were in the same group for the school trip," said Asha.

"And the time you broke into a locker and hid inside, so that you missed assembly."

"You know about that too?" Asha's eyes widened. "I have so many questions!"

"There is no time for—"

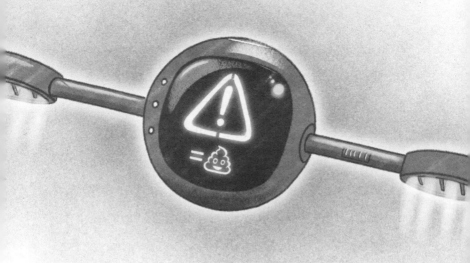

Drone was flashing a red light on her display, and flying frantically in a circle.

"Hey, Drone, you OK?" Asha went over to her.

"I have scanned 234 news sites from across the globe and 233 of them are confirming reports of sharks causing severe Internet disruption," said Drone. "The only website that didn't was droneracing.com, but they only talk about drone racing. Usually, I would check another 945 news sites, but ... my Internet connection is too slow right now."

Drone was trying to keep her voice calm, but Asha could tell that she was worried. Half of

Drone's functions relied on Internet access. Asha reached up and pulled the little machine close, hugging her tight.

"OMG!" Tumble narrowed his eyes, suddenly intrigued. "Drone won't be able to do anything without the Internet. She'll be like a phone without a signal, a bee without stripes, a bogey without..." He caught sight of Drone's display and cleared his throat. "Don't worry. Me and Asha will save the Internet. You can thank us later, Smellycopter."

Drone didn't reply, but her red flashing light was replaced by a bright yellow distress emoji.

"Tumble's right," Asha said, sounding more confident than she felt. "We can do this. We can sneak into Shelly Inc and get that file. Well, probably." Her voice trailed off at the end.

"It will be dangerous, Asha," warned Drone. "Shelly Inc has successfully prosecuted 100 per cent of intruders and—"

"Just to be clear," said Asha, turning away from Drone to Hedy. "You want me, Asha Joshi, to join the Children's Spy Agency and help save the whole Internet?"

"Affirmative. We have specially selected
you for a combination of your hacking skills,
intelligence, ingenuity, inquisitiveness, agility and
determination," replied Hedy. Asha still didn't
know what agility meant, but didn't want to
interrupt. "You must obey CSA protocols at all
times. These can be viewed in your CSA app."

Asha felt her tablet vibrate in her backpack.
She took it out and found a confirmation message
bobbing on her home screen:

MY MISSIONS | **MY TRAINING** | **MY INTEL**

WELCOME TO THE CSA

We're a top-secret children's spy agency.
We have agents all over the world, using their
skills to solve crimes, catch crooks and avoid
their chores at all costs.

Everyone in the CSA brings something new to the table – if you're reading this, it means you're just what we need.

Agents should think for themselves and question everything. If we wanted agents who followed orders without thinking, then we'd just send robots out into the field. We've got loads of them already. Some of them are really shiny. But we don't want that.

We want YOU, because you can think for yourself and figure out better, smarter and faster ways to do things.

4

| MY MISSIONS | MY TRAINING | MY INTEL |

? **Please follow these protocols when carrying out CSA missions.** ¿

PROTOCOL 1
Question everything

PROTOCOL 2
Think for yourself

PROTOCOL 3
Don't steal boats

PROTOCOL 4
Search for the truth

PROTOCOL 5
Trust your instincts

PROTOCOL 6
Charge your gadgets

PROTOCOL 7
█████████

PROTOCOL 8
Don't eat yellow snow, or anything bigger than your head

PROTOCOL 9
Remain calm

PROTOCOL 10
Abandon missions when instructed to

PROTOCOL 11
Be observant. Notice everything

PROTOCOL 12
Break problems down into logical steps

PROTOCOL 13
Be tenacious. If you can't find a way, create a new one

PROTOCOL 14
Don't hurt people, or anything else that might have feelings

<

For the complete list, <u>click here</u>

>

CODE OF CONDUCT

MY MISSIONS	MY TRAINING	MY INTEL

You're in charge. Sort of.

The CSA has no leader – we answer to each other. However, since we can't all be at the same place at the same time, we've programmed an AI decision-maker – Hedy – to gather intelligence, crunch data, and use logic to decide the best course of action.

CSA probation

To become a fully certified agent of the CSA, you must first pass a probation period. During this time, your performance will be carefully examined by Hedy. When on a mission you are expected to **(1)** cause minimal damage to property **(2)** cause minimal harm to others, and **(3)** ensure the CSA's identity remains top secret. Your probation may be extended if you do not follow our code of conduct.

Emergency contact

At the first available opportunity every agent must choose a CSA "Friend". This is a person outside the CSA who you trust to share your agent status with, and who we can call in an emergency. It could be your best friend, your sibling, a parent or guardian, but no pets (unless they can speak or code).

Your "Friend" will be allowed to know of our existence, but they will not have access to mission information, our hyper-advanced gadgets or our detection-proof jackets.

"If you follow CSA protocol, we anticipate you will be completely successful." The tangled wires of Hedy's lips twisted into a smile.

"Thanks, Hedy," said Asha, scrolling through the app. "I can honestly say I've never felt so comforted by a giant hologram."

"There is no time for comfort," said Hedy. "We have a free Internet at the moment, but it will not be long until Shelly takes it over. No government disaster plan has covered this eventuality. We are depending on you to break into Shelly Inc and get that file. Do you accept Mission Shark Bytes, Asha Joshi?"

Asha saw Drone still frantically trying to scan the Internet. Drone needed her. The CSA needed her. Did the whole world need her? Maybe, maybe not. But the Internet was definitely important, and Asha remembered how bad she'd felt when Anushka had read her diary. Privacy was important too.

She took a deep breath and nodded.

Chapter 7

--.. --- / -.. --- - / ... - .. -..-. --- / --- .- -.. --.

. - ... / ... .--. / ---- --- ... .-. / -.. --- ... .

11:12

"To break into Shelly Inc, you will need help, Asha Joshi. That's where the CSA's Department of Gadgets and Stink Bombs comes in. Our agents have invented some of the most advanced equipment in the world," said Hedy. "And the stink bombs really do stink."

"I require confirmation that none of the gadgets are weapons," Drone said.

"Affirmative. Weapons are strictly forbidden," Hedy replied.

"Noted." Drone vibrated in relief.

"Place your ear here to indicate your official consent to Mission Shark Bytes." Hedy turned into a scanner. Asha took a deep breath and pressed the side of her head against the hologram. A light travelled up and down the length of her ear before making an extremely strange beep. "Earprint confirmed. Agent Asha now live," Hedy said.

Wax: 10%
Shape: Unique
Heat: High

A compartment rose out of the floor. Asha rushed over and watched as it opened and revealed … three dusty books.

She'd been expecting grappling hooks or hoverboots or at least something with lasers.

"So am I supposed to … hit Shelly with a book?"

"Negative," said Hedy. "Weapons are forbidden, remember."

"Right, right." Asha nodded. "Knowledge is power! So I'll read the books ... like a bedtime story ... and send Shelly to sleep?"

Hedy flickered. "Have you ever been told the human idiom: never judge a book by its cover?" The voice paused for thirteen long seconds before continuing. "Hold your hologram card over one of them."

Asha did, and for a moment nothing happened. But then the cover slid up, revealing a large phone, twice the size of Asha's tablet. It looked like the ancient brick phones they used in really old movies.

"A satellite phone," said Drone approvingly. "It will work even if all the undersea and land Internet cables are destroyed."

Impatiently, Asha used her card to open the next book. It contained a water bottle. Her heart sinking a little, she opened the bottle's cap and found a hidden multitool. It might come in useful, she supposed. But it was still a bit boring.

Asha opened the third and final book, hoping for an invisibility device. Instead there was a very ordinary looking selfie stick.

"Now read the user manuals on the CSA app, Agent Asha," Hedy said.

Tumble immediately grabbed the selfie stick. "It is encrypted with Asha's fingerprints," Hedy warned Tumble. "It will only work for her."

MY MISSIONS	MY TRAINING	MY INTEL

What-A-Bottle

The What-A-Bottle can turn even the muddiest puddle water into clean drinking water. It's important to keep drinking out in the field. Also contains a state-of-the-art multitool.

Includes:
</> Screwdriver
</> Laser torch
</> Emergency dog whistle
</> Diamond cutter
</> There is no secret compartment

Satellite phone

Yes, it looks like a brick. But this phone can access the Internet from practically anywhere, by bouncing data off specialized CSA satellites in space. You can call us from the middle of the Atlantic Ocean, the top of Mount Everest, or even from the Torquay Train Tunnel Museum if you really wanted.

Agents should only use satellite Internet when there are no other options. Sending data into space is slower and less efficient than undersea cables.

❯

SECURITY ACTIVATED

DISCLAIMER: Everything on this page is highly confidential and NOT to be shared with anyone outside the CSA. If you are not the intended recipient of this briefing, destroy IMMEDIATELY.

MY MISSIONS   **MY TRAINING**   **MY INTEL**

Megafart Selfie Stick

To the untrained eye, this looks like a normal selfie stick. And it is. BUT if the built-in fingerprint scanner detects unknown fingerprints, the stick will unleash a powerful – and really pooey – stench gas, called a megafart.

Do not leave the megafart selfie stick lying around.

Specs:

</> Unleashes a pooey fart by default.

</> Can also release onion burps, garlic breath, and a spicy little something we call a pooclear pong.

</> Built from a super tough aluminium alloy. Resistant to corrosion, but gets very sticky if covered in jam.

</> Can be folded to look around corners.

</> Can be used to get a great angle for a selfie. No special activation is needed.

SEND GADGET INVENTIONS TO
THE DEPARTMENT OF GADGETS (THE DOG)

SUBMIT GADGET

Asha swiped the stick from Tumble before he could press anything.

"What?" he grumbled. "Good thing I've got all the gadgets I need right here." He waved his phone.

Hedy ignored him. "Please step into Area X, for your official outfitting."

The floor under Asha's feet lit up in fluorescent green. She followed the path to an X-shaped alcove in the wall. As she stepped inside, a green light filled the space. Asha saw robotic arms extending from either side of the wall, but then it became too bright to see anything at all.

Milliseconds later, the lights turned off and Asha found herself dressed in a dark bodysuit, with green lines on either side and padding on her elbows, knees and bum. She touched the material. It was unlike anything she had ever felt before.

"The bodysuit is sun, sweat and fart regulating," Hedy said. "Now there are 37 final words of warning, Agent Asha: Your mission is to get into Shelly Inc, download the file and upload it to our network. Nothing more. You have the makings of a

top agent, but our character evaluation shows that you may be reckless."

Asha opened her mouth to say something, but then she closed it again. There was no point arguing. The best way to prove herself to Hedy would be to ace the mission. "Got it."

"Good," said Hedy. "A vehicle will transport you to and from Shelly Inc. Please do not put your feet on the seats."

"Why? Are they ejector seats?" asked Asha.

"No," said Hedy. "We just had them cleaned. And remember, Shelly Belly is trying to bring down every Internet connection in the world. Sea first, then land, then satellites. Move fast or—" The hologram flickered, buzzed and then vanished entirely.

Asha gasped. "Hedy?" There was no reply.

"Another attack," whispered Drone.

Chapter 8

.-.. .. ... - . -- / - --- / .. -..- . / ---.. ... . .-
-- / .... .- -- ...

11:20

Asha's heart was thumping. She had just joined a secret intelligence agency. Now she had to break into a massive office. With lots of security. Then steal a top-secret file. To save the Internet. From fish.

It made no sense, but there was no time to waste. "Drone? Tumble? Grab the gadgets." She stuffed them in her backpack and motioned towards the tunnel entrance. "Let's go save the world's Internet."

"Or at least, the half of the world that had an Internet connection to begin with," Drone added.

The door slid open with a tap of Asha's holographic card and the three of them crawled through the tunnel. Another tap of the card and the shelf swung open back into the main library.

They raced outside. Asha was blinded by the sunlight and had to blink things back into focus. A woman with staring eyes bolted out of her front

door. She was wearing her sweater the wrong way round. "Is your Internet working?" she asked Asha, jabbing frantically at her phone screen. "I'm missing the latest episode of *Shelly by the Sea*."

Before Asha could reply, a man ran past with his hands on his head. "My MapApp just stopped working. I can't remember where I live!"

"Why is everyone freaking out because of a few connection issues?" asked Tumble, as he snapped a selfie. "Let me upload this and ... ARGH! CONNECTION ISSUES!"

"Never mind your selfies!" Drone was whirring with anxiety. "I won't be able to use search engines, send updates to Asha's parents or watch live drone racing!"

Asha caught sight of the news playing on a nearby billboard.

"It's official!" said the newsreader. "The government has just confirmed reports that our Internet cables are under attack from sharks. Hospitals are in chaos as patient data cannot be accessed. Air traffic control is offline, leaving all planes grounded. Dramatic scenes are being reported as the country comes to a standstill."

People were gathering around the billboard, their phones hanging uselessly by their sides. The reporter paused and held his hand up to his earpiece. "Wait! News just in!" His voice started shaking with excitement. "Teenage tech entrepreneur Shelly Belly is launching a new Internet service called ShellyNet. Let's go live to her announcement."

As Asha watched, the camera cut to Shelly Inc. Shelly was stepping out of a large helicopter, onto a bright green lawn. Her white hair gleamed in the sun. Amanda, her monkey-panda hybrid, was wrapped around her shoulders.

Shelly stopped, straightened her sleeves and started speaking to the crowd of reporters. "As you know, our Internet cables are breaking. And so is my heart. At Shelly Inc, we know that the Internet is a basic human right, and I shudder at the thought of a world without it." She shook her head and the crowd beside Asha murmured in

agreement. "In moments of global crisis, we come
together as a family. And as part of that family,
Shelly Inc is here to help."

Shelly paused and looked straight at the camera.
It felt as though she was looking right into Asha's
eyes. "It seems that cables that carry 99 per cent of
the global Internet have been attacked by sharks,
and suffered catastrophic damage. Shelly Inc
has developed shark-proof cables, and since this
morning, I have been helping our engineers by laying
these new cables around the country with my own

two hands." She gestured towards the helicopter, flashing her perfectly white teeth as she smiled.

"Our new service is called ShellyNet and I'm humbled to announce that it has just gone live. It will cost £20 a week to access three websites, and an additional £5 for three priority websites, including FriendTrend and FaceSpace. To sign up, all you will need is an official ID document and a credit or debit card. This is incredible value to use the Internet: a service that none of us deserves to live without! It's the least Shelly Inc can do to help our brothers and sisters around the world to stay online."

The camera returned to the studio in time to catch the newsreader high-fiving the weatherman, before he cleared his throat and picked up his tablet. "And in other news…"

Asha looked up and down the street. Hedy was right. Shelly was up to something. There's no way she could've invented shark-proof cables in less than 24 hours.

Warning: pizzas cause diarrhoea

That might not be true, but you believed it! That's why fake news is so dangerous. Fake news articles are designed to trick people into believing something that might not be fact. It's hard to spot fake news – computers can make fake images, fake voices and fake videos. A computer could make a video of Santa Claus farting in a polar bear's mouth – or something even worse. CSA agents must be able to separate fake news and real news. Question everything, even if it looks like it's real.

How to spot fake news:

1
Question the person who wrote it.
Do they know what they're talking about?

2
Is the story being reported anywhere else?

3
Agents should also check that images, articles, voice messages, text messages, online polls, online comments and even emails are authentic - they can all be faked.

"I bet she wasn't laying cables this morning. Maybe she used that helicopter to transport the sharks and…" Asha suddenly remembered what they were waiting for. "Where's the CSA vehicle?" she said to Drone and Tumble, trying to drown out the sound of the crowd chanting Shelly Belly's name. "And how will we know what it looks like?"

"I bet it's something cool," said Tumble. "Like a hoverbike. Or a hoverlimo. Or a hot-air balloon!"

Asha wasn't sure what to expect, given that she'd just been briefed by a plate of eggs. "Maybe it's not coming," she said after a moment.

Almost immediately, a colourful van pulled up in front of them. Its sides were covered with pictures of ice cream, glistening with chocolate sprinkles. But it was playing the strangest ice-cream van music that Asha had ever heard. Instead of a catchy jingle, it was short, sharp, stop-start notes, like a woodpecker playing the keyboard.

"What on earth is that?" Asha put her hands over her ears.

"That's not music," said Drone. "It's Morse code."

"Morse code?" Asha shouted over the noise. "Ace! Drone, display the Morse code key, so we can work it out." She pushed her lip up to touch her nose while she translated the sounds. "It says ... ASHA GET IN!"

At that moment, the side of the van slid open, revealing a shiny chrome interior. "Welcome, Agent Asha," said an electronic voice.

The inside of the ice-cream van was just as incredible as the secret library base. The van was self-driving so Asha was free to look around at all the displays and flashing lights. There was camera footage of every angle of the street outside the van. Other screens showed live streams of CSA agents from all over the world – Ghana, Estonia and Brazil – all talking to one another via a blinking array of satellite connections.

Tumble was posing in front of his phone, when Asha's tablet started buzzing in her backpack. An alert flashed on Drone's screen. It was an invitation to join a secure satellite connection. Drone accepted first, and as soon as she did, she

started pinging with notifications. "We've been away for 62 minutes. Your parents have a 92 per cent likelihood of wondering where you are as it is approaching lunchtime. Suspicion levels were already raised when you said that you were going to the library."

Asha had almost forgotten. "Ugh, good point. Run Program 719."

Drone hesitated. "My nannybot programming says that the correct course of action is to call your parents and tell them where you are."

"Run your Special Circumstances Emergency Override," said Asha. "I programmed that for you months ago, remember?"

She had reprogrammed Drone's decision-making algorithms to allow for unexpected situations. "This is a special circumstance. Mum and Dad would approve if they knew I was saving the Internet!"

Drone let out a long robot-sigh. "Fine. I will run Program 719. But only this once."

She rang Mum's mobile. Asha's dad picked up.

"Hi, Nikhil," said Drone, in a human voice. "It's me, Temi. How are you? I'm just checking in to let you know Asha wants to have lunch here and stay for a sleepover."

Drone's voice sounded exactly like Demola's mum, Temitayo. The last time she'd stayed over, Asha had secretly recorded her.

"Ah, Auntie Temi. Lovely to hear from you. Sure, Asha can stay, but only if she promises to finish her circus project," said her dad. So predictable.

"Of course. I'll make sure our terrible two both do their homework!" said the recording of Temitayo. "And go to bed on time."

"Fantastic!" said Asha's dad. "Wonderful! We'll see her tomorrow then." Easy.

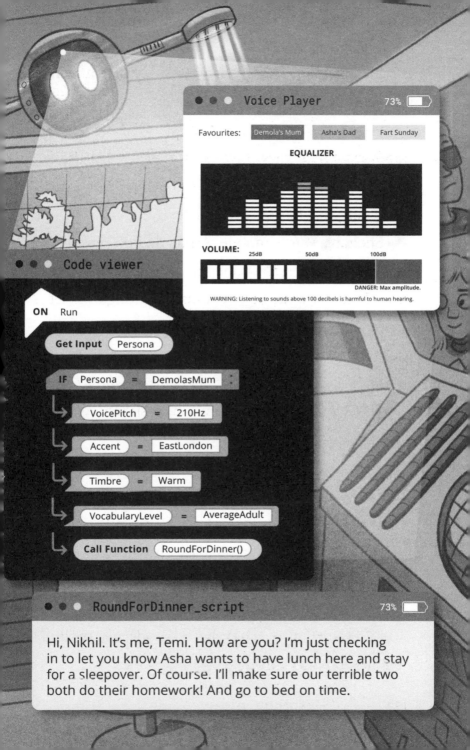

Voice Player 73%

Favourites: Demola's Mum | Asha's Dad | Fart Sunday

EQUALIZER

VOLUME: 25dB 50dB 100dB

DANGER: Max amplitude.

WARNING: Listening to sounds above 100 decibels is harmful to human hearing.

Code viewer

```
ON Run

Get Input  Persona

IF  Persona  =  DemolasMum :

    VoicePitch  =  210Hz

    Accent  =  EastLondon

    Timbre  =  Warm

    VocabularyLevel  =  AverageAdult

    Call Function  RoundForDinner()
```

RoundForDinner_script 73%

Hi, Nikhil. It's me, Temi. How are you? I'm just checking in to let you know Asha wants to have lunch here and stay for a sleepover. Of course. I'll make sure our terrible two both do their homework! And go to bed on time.

Chapter 9

.- .-.. .-- .- ....- ... / ... . -.... ... --. / ---. ---
... .-. / -... --- ... .

12:25

Asha looked through the van's one-way windows, and watched the greys and browns of London turn into green fields. Asha knew that Shelly Inc was based somewhere just outside the city, but she didn't know exactly where. The van began to weave its way up a hill, and when it turned around a corner, Asha spotted something glittering in the distance. They'd arrived.

The Shelly Inc building was all shiny steel and mirror glass – it was dazzling. This was where all of Shelly's apps and products were designed,

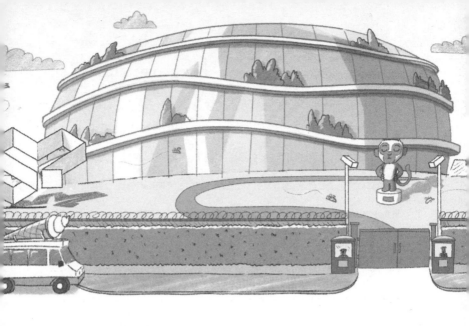

built, prototyped and tested. If the rumours were
true, there were also highly confidential research
bunkers and a digital zoo on site. The building was
famous for its fun workspaces, which looked more
like playgrounds than offices. Asha had always
wanted to try out the ShellySlide which connected
the top and bottom floors.

Asha stepped out of the van, grabbing her
backpack. She began walking towards the sparkling
building, with Drone hovering and Tumble trotting
at her side. They had to shield their eyes against
the glare from the windows.

"Right then, how are we going to get inside?" Asha asked them.

"We could pretend to work there?" Tumble suggested, looking up at the huge, blank panels of the front gate. Security guards dressed in grey were stationed in little booths on either side.

"Unwise," replied Drone. "From the data analysis I carried out on the journey here, Shelly Inc has 98,771 employees, but there weren't any hamsters on the team. Besides, they'll probably use eyeball scanning."

"Sweet!" said Tumble.

Drone sighed. "Not sweet. We don't have eyeballs, Tumble. We're robots."

As the pair began arguing about eyeballs and retinal scanning, Asha began to make a plan for getting past the guards. She ran through all of the possible options and some impossible ones too.

Then she thought about the spy shows she'd watched on HypePipe. "I bet there's more than one entrance. There must be a back way for delivery lorries. If we could hide inside a lorry, we might be able to sneak past security. Let's go check it out."

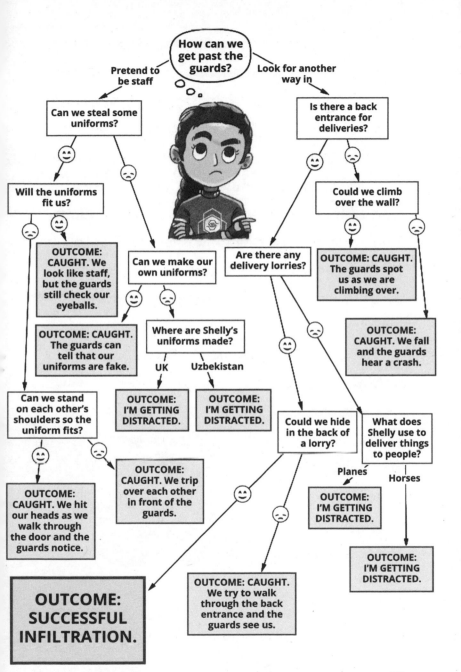

They crept around the edge of the fence but they didn't get far. A slick black quadcopter with a red warning light immediately flew up to them. "STEP AWAY FROM THE PERIMETER," it ordered.

Drone hovered steadily in the air. She wasn't worried by a poor quality, low-spec security drone. Tumble, on the other hand, was far less relaxed. He froze and tried to look as much like a toy as possible. Asha picked Tumble up and cuddled him close.

"He's gone into panic mode," Drone buzzed.

Asha was busy thinking. She had fooled plenty of grown-ups by pretending to be stupid and cute. Maybe the same

tactic would work on robots. "Sorry," she said to the security drone in her most babyish voice. "We're lost."

The drone paused in mid-air and scanned her. "Situation normal," it whirred and hovered away.

Tumble checked that the drone was safely out of sight again before springing back to life in Asha's arms. "Good thing I was here to scare that copter off," he announced, planting himself on Asha's shoulder and pointing forward. "Now let's go and break in!"

They carried on walking round the fence, ducking whenever they saw a CCTV camera, until Asha found what she'd been looking for: the back entrance. Like the front gate, security guards sat in two little booths on either side of the gleaming silver bars.

Asha watched as an orange lorry with the Shelly Inc logo drove towards the gates. As the lorry approached, it slowed down to pass under a metal arch. A robotic arm moved slowly above the lorry, bathing it in a red light. "NO THREAT

DETECTED," boomed an electronic voice. A green light flashed in the security guard's booth, and he waved the lorry through.

"It's a scanner," said Drone. "It shares many characteristics with those commonly found in airports. If we hide in a lorry, they'll catch us immediately."

Asha had a determined look in her eye. "Not if I can connect to the scanner and hack it. I just need to get close."

Before Drone could protest, Asha had dropped to her hands and knees, and was crawling through the mud and bushes towards the scanner. The plastic box containing the machine's circuits was hidden within reach of the bush. Asha pulled out her new What-A-Bottle with the hidden screwdrivers. Within seconds, she had opened the scanner's plastic casing.

"Aha! The serial port. Nice." Asha tapped a little trapezium-shaped socket that had nine gold pins. Then she connected her tablet to it and loaded up a terminal emulator. This program would allow

her to give the scanner new instructions. As she scanned each line of code, all the noise around her disappeared. It was just Asha and her screen.

"I'll reprogram the scanner," she whispered to herself. "At the moment, the alarms are programmed to sound if there's anything suspicious in the back of the lorry." Within minutes, she'd found the bit of code that she wanted to tweak, rewritten it, and rebooted the system. "Now none of the alarms will go off, even if there's something highly suspicious in the back of the lorry, like me, my nannybot and robot hamster!"

```
01    #This program scans lorries and cars. If something suspicious is found
02    by the scanner, then an alarm will sound. You need to be very careful
03    to code the correct number for the alarm you want. Especially since
04    001 plays the "no danger alarm" and 010 sounds all the alarms!#
05
06    //Warning: Alarm 010 plays ALL THE ALARMS.
07    //The scanner will use the table to figure out which alarm to play.
08
09    Alarm.Type
10    [No threat detected] 001
11    [Intruders detected] 002
12    [Journalists detected] 003
13    [Off-grid human detected] 004
14    [Piranhas detected] 005
15    [Stink bomb detected] 006
16    [Martians detected] 007
17    [T-Rex detected] 008
18    [Zombies detected] 009
19    [Sound all alarms] 010
20
21
22    ON [Scanner Run]
23    IF [Stink bomb] detected
24       > Play [Alarm.006]
25    ELSE IF [Intruders] detected
26       > Play [Alarm.002]
27    ELSE
28       > Play [Alarm.001]
29
30    //When the scanner runs, if it detects a stink bomb, then play Alarm 006.
31    // Or if it detects an intruder, play Alarm 002.
32    // If there is no threat detected, then play Alarm 001 to let the security
33    guard know everything is OK.
34    // Alarm 010 sounds all the alarms, so be careful when editing the code.
```

"Tumble, Drone, we need to be ready." Asha beckoned them over. "The next time a lorry stops, we're jumping in the back and staying very quiet!"

"The radiation from the scanner is at acceptable levels so long as we don't spend more than 24 hours in it," Drone replied, scanning the equipment. "In fact, we will be exposed to less radiation than eating a hundred—"

The low hum of an engine interrupted Drone.

Another lorry was approaching the scanner. Perfect. Asha ran out of the bushes, opened the doors and scrambled into the back. Tumble clung to her jumpsuit and Drone followed on silent mode. Apart from a slither of light creeping in under the door and the glow of Asha's tablet, it was very dark inside.

The lorry moved into the scanner.

"NO THREAT DETECTED," the voice boomed. Asha breathed a sigh of relief.

And then, suddenly:

"INTRUDERS DETECTED!"

"JOURNALISTS DETECTED!"

"OFF-GRID HUMAN DETECTED!"

"PIRANHAS DETECTED!"

"What's happening?" Asha began to panic as the voice kept going. She scrolled frantically through the code. "Oh no, there's a bug!"

"OMG! Where?" Tumble jumped onto Asha's shoulder. "Not another one!"

"No, Tumble. A computer bug. Remember? Jam sandwiches?" Tumble's face was blank. "I've accidentally programmed it to play all of the possible alarms, instead of playing nothing at all."

"STINK BOMB DETECTED!"

From the back of the lorry, Asha heard shouts, as the security guard came running. Asha needed to fix this before they were caught. Time seemed to slow down as she ran through the code.

"You seriously think I've got piranhas and a stink bomb in here?" the lorry driver shouted. "Ridiculous. Your scanner's broken, pal."

"MARTIANS DETEC—!"

```
01   #This program scans lorries and cars. If something suspicious is found
02   by the scanner, then an alarm will sound. You need to be very careful
03   to code the correct number for the alarm you want. Especially since 001
04   plays the "no danger alarm" and 010 sounds all the alarms!#
05
06   //Warning: Alarm 010 plays ALL THE ALARMS.
07   //The scanner will use the table to figure out which alarm to play.
08
09   Alarm.Type
10   [No threat detected] 001
11   [Intruders detected] 002
12   [Journalists detected] 003
13   [Off-grid human detected] 004
14   [Piranhas detected] 005
15   [Stink bomb detected] 006
16   [Martians detected] 007
17   [T-Rex detected] 008
18   [Zombies detected] 009
19   [Sound all alarms] 010
20
21   ON [Scanner Run]
22   IF [Stink bomb] detected
23     > Play [Alarm.006]
24   ELSE IF [Intruders] detected
25     > Play [Alarm.010]
26   ELSE
27     > Play [Alarm.001]
```

The message cut off, mid-word, as Asha finished debugging.

"Right," said the lorry driver in the sudden silence. "Let's try this again."

Asha heard her climb back into the cab, and felt the lorry reversing out of the scanner. When it moved forward again, the voice announced "NO THREAT DETECTED," and then fell silent.

"I should still check in there," protested the guard.

Asha's eyes widened. She glanced around the lorry. There were tubes of waterproof sealant and bundles of colourful cables, but there was nowhere for them to hide. Tumble was on the floor in panic mode again, and Drone's warning lights were flashing red. Asha held her breath. How could she have made such a simple mistake?

The lorry driver spoke again. "No way. You're wasting my time. Or do you want to explain to Shelly B why her delivery is behind schedule?"

"Uh … mmmm… Well … the thing is… No." The guard sounded uncomfortable.

The truck lurched forwards as the driver started it up again. Asha heard the gate slide open, and then the lorry trundled into Shelly Inc.

"WE'RE IN! WE'VE DONE IT." Asha whisper-shouted the words. She felt a strange mixture of adrenaline, adventure and something else... Guilt? Fear? She'd never broken the law before. At least, never knowingly. Even though Hedy had said that the CSA worked with governments all over the world, Asha wondered if she was making a mistake. This was different from skipping assembly. She closed her eyes, and imagined a warm cup of chai and a head rub from Dad...

"How are you feeling, Asha?" asked Drone. "You have not eaten in 2 hours and 19 minutes. My facial scans suggest that—"

"I'm fine," Asha snapped, opening her eyes, and pulling a banana out of her backpack. It was too late to turn back now. And besides, they were following Hedy's instructions and breaking the law for a very good reason.

They were saving the Internet.

Chapter 10

.--. .- ... .--. --- .-. -.. / .. ... / -- --- - / .- / --. --- --- -.. / .--. .- ... .--. --- .-. -..

12:49

In the darkness of the lorry, a warning flashed up on Drone's display. It was an alert to join ShellyNet WiFi, if they agreed to the terms and conditions.

Asha narrowed her eyes, remembering what Hedy had told her about Shelly Inc. "Let's not join the WiFi. I don't think we should agree to these."

Drone was silent but her loading wheel was working overtime. Usually she was reluctant to let Asha sign up for anything unless she was at least 75 per cent in agreement with the terms and conditions. But there was no CSA backup satellite

Welcome to ShellyNet

SHELLY INC

To access our free WiFi, simply agree to the terms and conditions below.

☐ I agree

Click here

Terms and conditions:

Use of the A. Manda Cloud grants Shelly Inc complete access to your data, ownership of your information and the right to use uploaded images for any purpose.

Shelly will know everything about you, and she'll get ownership of your name and your address. She can do whatever she wants with this information. She can even print your face on a constipation relief tablet box and there's nothing you can do about it.

Risk = Asha's face can be used anywhere! Even here!

POOPAGEN

For fast constipation relief

24

connection for Drone in Shelly Inc. Without WiFi, Drone wouldn't be able to access half her functions, including location services.

"On this one occasion, I calculate that it is safer to break the rules," she said eventually. Robot-sighing, Drone signed up with a fake email account.

Asha and Tumble looked at each other in amazement.

"We're stopping!" said Tumble, clenching his tiny paws into fists. "Let's roll. Time to show Shelly what we're made of."

"Absolutely not," said Drone. "It's much more logical to wait and listen, to see if—"

Tumble jumped back onto Asha's shoulder and the two leapt out of the back of the lorry before Drone could finish her sentence. They were in a huge underground loading bay with orange Shelly Inc lorries parked everywhere. Robotic arms on giant wheels were loading crates into the back of the empty lorries. Asha and Tumble dived behind the first crate they could see. Drone's display dimmed unhappily, but there was no way she was going to let Asha go into Shelly Inc on her own.

Asha looked around. On one wall a large screen displayed a map of Shelly Inc. Hedy had said that the ShellyServer was located in Shelly's office. That was at the other end of the building, on the floor above them, only two corridors away from the world-famous and much FaceSpaced ShellySlide. Asha felt excitement bubble inside.

FIRE EVACUATION PLAN

shelly Inc

YOU ARE HERE

She pointed at some metal doors at the far side of the car park. "There's the lift. Chalo!"

"Too dangerous," beeped Drone. "The floor numbers are changing so there must be people using it."

"Don't be such a scaredycopter, Drone! We're not going to get caught." Tumble waved his tiny paws. "Not with my mad skills!" He kicked at the air and slipped off Asha's shoulder, landing with a crash beside a crate. Luckily, the noise was covered up by the robots loading the lorries.

Drone was right. It wasn't safe to use the lift. Asha scanned the car park. They needed another way to get into Shelly's office.

"Look!" She pointed to the base of a wall. "That's an air vent." She ran over to it, hoping her new CSA bodysuit would help her blend into her surroundings. She opened her backpack, flipped the cap of her What-A-Bottle and within seconds was using her screwdriver to unscrew the cover panel. She stuck her head inside the vent and found a maintenance map stuck to the inside. It looked as though one of the vents led up to the floor above and then all the way across to Shelly's office. So far so good.

Asha looked around then squeezed inside. The vent was designed for maintenance bots and was only just large enough for her. It was hard to get a grip on the metal surface, so she pressed her back against one side and started edging upwards with her feet. Drone hovered behind with Tumble balanced on her wing.

Five stomach-pinching minutes later, a new air-vent path opened on their right. Breathing a sigh of relief, Asha stopped climbing and started crawling forwards, stopping at each junction to make sure she had remembered the route correctly.

Every few metres, a ventilation grille would give them a glimpse of what was happening below inside Shelly Inc. They passed over a huge workshop where engineers were building rows of dark objects that looked like small aeroplanes.

Then they crawled over a gym, where sweating employees were pedalling on exercise bikes, while typing on laptops at the same time. Electronic music pumped through the wall-speakers. "Bliss! Unity! Big! Motivate! Reach! The! Sales! Sky!" yelled the instructor.

There were endless yoga studios and smoothie stations. As Asha stopped and took a sip of water she listened in on one of the meetings. "Hey, teamies! Hold up!" The speaker was pointing at a smart board. "We need to complete our KPIs and OKRs and FYIs and IDKs before 1 p.m. remember? Or we won't get our Daily Poo Bonus Break. TEAMWORK IS ... monitored heavily and assessed every minute. You wouldn't want to let the whole team down by wasting time farting, would you?"

"Let's keep going," said Asha, crawling a little bit faster. Shelly Inc wasn't *quite* how she had imagined.

Meanwhile, Tumble was swinging off the pipes and jumping from grille to grille. "Ouch!" muttered Asha, as he kicked her in the head for the third time. She looked down and stopped suddenly. "Drone, look at this!"

Below was another room full of computer screens. But what had caught Asha's attention was a beautiful butterfly fluttering through the air. Only the flashing blue lights on its antennae gave it away as a robot. A woman was controlling it using a device, while two

people scribbled notes on a smart board.

"Bluetooth test 3006 has been successful," announced one.

Asha narrowed her eyes. "Wow, 3,006 tests is a lot – even for me. What are they testing for? And why is Shelly interested in Bluetooth?"

"Bluetooth doesn't require the Internet," replied Drone. "So it's unlikely to be linked to ShellyNet. It's too short-range." She sounded nervous. "But what if it's spyware and that bot has a camera? Let's keep going."

Asha was grateful now for the knee-padding in her bodysuit. They kept crawling until they found themselves looking down on a room that made Asha stop and blink. It was one of the workspaces where Shelly often filmed her FaceSpace videos. The floor was covered in grass, and plants tumbled down the walls. A rainbow-striped slide spiralled down through the floor.

"Can we go on the ShellySlide?" asked Tumble, bouncing up and down. "I've always wanted to. Come on Ashaface, *please* times a thousand million zillion!"

"Nope," said Asha. "But I reckon the slide is near to Shelly's office. I think we're really close!"

She was fascinated by the room. There were no desks. Instead, people sat in egg-shaped pods, which dangled from the ceiling like gigantic neon insect cocoons. Everyone was tapping away on at least one laptop. No one was talking. Bots zipped around with trays of smoothies and snacks.

"Amateurs," muttered Drone at Asha's heels. Drone was always disdainful of delivery bots. Maybe she was secretly scared of becoming one.

Asha wondered what it would be like to work at Shelly Inc. Even though everyone was smiling, something felt funny. They looked the same, walked the same and talked the same. Dad had always told her to trust her gut – and her gut was telling her to get out of here. Despite the bright colours and adventure-playground furniture, Shelly Inc didn't seem to be any fun at all.

"This place gives me the creeps," she said to Drone and Tumble, as she started to move through the vent again. "Let's find the file and get out of here."

Just as Asha was thinking her knees couldn't possibly crawl any further, she looked down through the grille and saw a room where almost everything was made out of glass.

There were no slides or cocoons. A painting of what looked like a rectangle trying to eat two triangles hung above a desk that was bigger than Asha's bed. A flat-screen monitor glinted on the desk. Underneath the desk was a large, black box, with a line of flashing lights down one side. SHELLYSERVER was printed across it in bright orange.

They'd found it.

Chapter 11

.---. .-. ... .-- --- .-. -.. / .. ... / .-. . .- .--.
.--. .--- / -. --- - / .- / --. --- --- -.. / .--. .-
... .-- --- .-. ...

13:11

Asha started feeling around the vent, searching for
a way to open the grille. Drone's torch revealed a
small rectangle of metal rising up from the smooth
ceiling. Asha saw it was a digital lock, with the
numbers one to ten neatly displayed in a grid. This
server was the heart of the organization, the jewel
in the crown, the cheese on the pizza, so it made
sense that Shelly had used her tightest security
and a complex encryption to stop anyone from
accessing it.

Or so she thought.

She hadn't planned for secret agents like Asha. Asha had spent the last eleven years making (and breaking) gadgets, apps and locks. And perfecting the tiniest lines of code had given Asha an amazing attention to detail. The first thing she spotted on the lock? Dirty smears. Someone had recently opened it. When she tilted her head to the side and Drone shone the torch at just the right angle, it was easy to tell which keys had been pressed.

"Drone?" whispered Asha. "Can you run the Number Generation Program and try every combination of 1, 4, 6, 7 and 9?"

Steadied by Tumble, Drone was able to extend a metal arm all the way through the grille. Moving with the kind of speed and precision only achieved by robots, she tapped through the 3,125 possible combinations of the dirty numbers. After thirteen seconds, the lock display flashed green and the grille slowly opened.

Without thinking about the distance from the ceiling to the floor, Asha jumped into the room

below. She landed on a carpet so soft and thick that it reminded her of a marshmallow. Tumble followed, bouncing a few times, before lying on his back and spreading his arms like he was making a snow angel. Drone glided down and hovered above Shelly's desk.

Asha went over to Drone and ran her fingers over the surface of the desk. A glass of water sat on a glass coaster. She sat down on the glass chair and the screen in front of her flashed into life. Was it activated by pressure on the seat? A user called Ricardo Kon Carney was still logged in.

"It's #TimeForT from the office today," Tumble interrupted Asha's thoughts. He had pulled his phone out of his pouch and was happily vlogging away. "Welcome to my workspace. Today's hot project: a carpet angel. Kind of a snow angel, but on a carpet. Next big thing? Like if you agree.

Admiring the painting on the wall? Tumble original, do not steal."

Drone snatched the phone. "Tumble, we are here undercover. If you post you will give away our location!" she snapped.

Asha was struggling to gather her thoughts. She pulled out her tablet and plugged it into a port on the side of the ShellyServer. A message flashed up on her screen: THIS IS A PRIVATE SERVER. AUTHORIZED PERSONNEL ONLY. PLEASE SELECT YOUR USERNAME.

Asha scrolled through the list of names, from

Milo De Coda to Nastia Nabakova, until she reached the one she wanted: Ricardo Kon Carney. She typed in the name and waited as a loading wheel whirred on her screen.

Then a message flashed up that made Asha bite her lower lip: TYPE YOUR PASSWORD HERE.

"LOL!" Drone's version of snort-laughter sounded like a drum. "Humans have such sophisticated security systems, but allow the most basic errors in judgement to occur. Weak and exposed passwords have, since 1961—"

"What are you talking about?" Asha asked. Then she followed Drone's gaze to a neon orange sticky note on the desk: RKC PW: #il0vedeadlin3s.

"Boom!" Asha grinned.

She entered the password and a second later, some green text appeared: ACCESS GRANTED. WELCOME BACK, RICARDO.

Thousands of files flashed across the screen of her tablet. Asha's eyes widened. The Operation DeepWater file wasn't going to be easy to find.

She booted up a search program and typed in the

filename. The loading wheel began to whir again.

"Why is it taking so long?" Drone was flying in small circles, her eyes flashing yellow. The risk of being caught was sending her warning systems into overdrive.

"Mmmm … about that…" said Asha, trying to stay calm. "I can't find the file. I've run the search I always use, but it doesn't look like it's here."

"But it must be!" Drone said desperately. "Hedy was clear: there is a file called Operation DeepWater saved locally on Shelly's computer system." For the last part, Drone played a recording of Hedy's voice. "Have you tried—"

"I know, I know! But maybe the CSA was wrong or maybe Shelly has … er … deleted it," Asha said, her stomach churning. "This is my sixth search!"

Drone looked at Asha's tablet. The loading wheel had been replaced by an error message: FILE NOT FOUND.

"What do we do now?" asked Drone. "Should I activate Panic Mode?"

"QUIET!" shouted Tumble. Then he whispered, "There are people outside."

MY MISSIONS	MY TRAINING	MY INTEL

? Would you like your parents to read your conversations? Or a robot to steal your secret files? Then you need to come up with a secure password. Follow these simple steps to upgrade your cybersecurity. **¿**

STEP 1

Come up with a word that isn't obviously connected to you. Made-up words are even better. Don't use any of these:

</> Obvious names *(your name, your pet's, your brother's, your friend's)*
</> Obvious places *(favourite holiday, where you were born, your street)*

A good example: floopysaurus

STEP 2

Include some numbers and symbols like @ * < ! to help confuse hacker robots. Y0U C4N 3V3N WR173 L1K3 7H15.

A good example: f100py5@uru5!

STEP 3

Have a biscuit. You deserve a reward for creating your very own non-stupid password.

Note: never tell your password to anyone, never write it down and never leave it stuck to the side of your device.

Chapter 12

--- · / ·- ·-· · / ··· --- ···· ···· ·· · / -·· · · ··

13:15

"The country has lost it," exclaimed an excited male voice. "It's just like the Iceland experiment! People have no choice but to sign up for ShellyNet. The secret plan is working better than we thought! You're totes an IRL genius."

"Secret plan?" responded a silky female voice that Asha instantly recognized. "Ricardo, are you talking about my plan to bring the Internet – a fundamental human right – to those who need it most, for only a very small cost? If so, then yes, it's definitely working. Am I a genius? I mean, I'd never say so myself, and it doesn't matter that I'm the youngest CEO ever on Falcon's Rich List."

"Yeah, that's what I meant. Can we cover the third SAP phase in your office, Shells? The first two operations have been totes amaze. Twenty cables have now been disabled and we're scheduled to depart for the final SAP in approx twenty minutes."

Asha had crouched behind Shelly's desk. The glass made it useless as a hiding place, but did give her a good view of the office. She saw two teenagers both dressed in white shirts and perfectly cut jeans that looked casual and expensive at the same time. Shelly's short, white hair gleamed even more brightly than it did in photos, while Ricardo had thick-rimmed glasses and a topknot. Amanda, the monkey-panda, was in her usual spot on the trillionaire's shoulders.

Asha couldn't believe she was this close to THE Shelly Belly. She'd seen her face on the news, in *Cabled* magazine, on the side of smart buses ... everywhere, really. She'd even dreamed about meeting her. Now Asha was metres away from her, but instead of chatting about artificially intelligent toilets that can find gold in poo, she had illegally broken into her office. This wasn't quite how she had imagined their meeting.

Asha looked across the fluffy carpet at Shelly's trainers. They were white and looked almost unworn. One of them was emblazoned with a logo. Underneath the logo, a small orange rectangle was set into the heel. Was there a picture of a shark in the rectangle? Asha thought it looked like part of the shoe's design, but when she looked again, there was something odd about it. It seemed to stick out from the rest of the shoe.

Asha held her breath. Was that what she thought it was?

Drone had been looking too. A string of letters ran silently across her screen: *USB*. Asha nudged Tumble and pointed at it. Tumble looked frantically from Asha to Drone, trying to work out what was going on.

Shelly stood still for a moment, listening to her in-ear phone. "That was our sales update, Ricky," she said, smiling. "Five hundred thousand people have signed up for ShellyNet in the last hour, and more than 50 per cent of them have purchased ShellyNet Gold, giving them free access to over three websites. It's so humbling that we are helping people get back online."

Ricardo giggled and tried to high-five Shelly, but she just smiled some more and stared at his hand until he lowered it again.

Asha's heart was racing. What if the CSA's intelligence was wrong about the server? She thought of her grandma, Dadi-Ji, who hid her most expensive jewellery and a month's supply of coriander in ice-cream tubs in the freezer because no burglar would ever look there.

If you thought about it, of course Shelly wouldn't store top-secret plans on her normal server, where they could be accessed by any of her 98,771 employees if they tried hard enough. What if ... what if she kept them somewhere else ... somewhere much harder for anyone to get to ... in a specially designed trainer. Then she'd always be right on top of her most important data and no one would ever think to look there!

Shelly was hiding things in plain sight. The DeepWater file must be on that USB. But how could Asha get to it? Shelly was standing on the opposite side of the room, and Asha knew they only had moments before they were discovered. She made eyes at Drone and Tumble, motioning towards Shelly's shoe with her chin.

She took a deep breath. For a split second, she

imagined curling up on the sofa with one of Demola's cheese and marmite toasties. But she was part of something much bigger now, much more spy than she'd ever imagined. She couldn't chicken out on her first real mission. She'd prove herself to the CSA. She was going to get that file, whatever it took.

Maybe Tumble could help? After all, he was trainer-height. Asha turned to him, ready to mouth instructions, only to find him trying to take a selfie with Shelly in the background. He pressed the camera button.

CLICK. The noise filled the silent office.

"What was that?" asked Ricardo.

Asha watched as four white trainers headed towards them. On one of them, the orange USB was now clearly visible, set into the side of the heel. And the logo was *definitely* a shark. But there was nowhere to go and there was nowhere to hide.

"Ooh, look. Ricky, we have a visitor! Hello, sweetie!" Shelly bent down, and looked directly into Asha's eyes. Her eyes were neither cold nor warm, and she spoke softly, in an almost-whisper. "How did you get in here?"

"I've lost my mummy! Have you seen her?" Asha used her baby voice and blinked innocently up at Shelly. Tumble opened his eyes very wide, and attempted his cutest toy face.

Ricardo rolled his eyes. "Not again! I don't know why the team keeps bringing their children into work. My assistant found a baby in his drawer the other day. So basic." He focused on Asha again. "I don't know where Mummy is, but when I find her, we'll need to have a very short conversation!"

Shelly spotted Drone trying to keep still under the desk. "Wow. That's one out-of-date nannybot!"

Immediately, Drone flew within inches of Shelly's face, meeting her gaze. "Actually, I have been custom-modified with highly advanced, state-of-the-art..." Drone saw Asha's pleading look. "Er … I mean … nannybot cannot process. Please upgrade."

But it was too late. Ricardo had spotted Asha's tablet, still plugged into the ShellyServer. "Looks like Mummy is an actual data thief," he snarled. "Though you've got to admire her tactics. Child labour. Excellent!"

"It might not be Mummy," Shelly said, grabbing hold of Drone and shaking her. "Tell me, sweetie. Who sent you? Who are you working for? It's OK, you can trust me. I'm not upset."

This wasn't good. Time to get creative. What had the CSA protocol said about cover stories?

"You got me," said Asha, flinging herself out from under the desk. "I'm Sophie Deen from Unicorn Box. We're a new tech start-up. Let go of

Drone. She's a touch-sensitive bomb!"

Shelly hesitated and loosened her grip on Drone, who flew out of reach.

"Tick, tick, tick, I'm a time bomb," Drone said in a monotone.

"IT'S #TIMEFORT, SHELLY!" Tumble burst out from under the desk. He slid across the carpet on his little hamster belly, crashing abruptly into Shelly's feet. Everyone was stunned, giving Tumble just enough time to grab hold of the orange USB. With a tug of his paw, it came free. Asha heard a high-pitched beep. Shelly tried to kick out at Tumble and missed, but Amanda was quicker.

The monkey-panda swung down from Shelly's shoulder and began to chase Tumble around the room. Tumble made a flying leap for Shelly's desk, his paws skidding across the glass surface. Amanda jumped in front of him, her long tail swishing

behind her, blocking his way back to Asha.

Tumble stopped next to the water glass and pulled his paws into his best karate pose. "Take that, Panda-Monkey!" he cried, kicking the glass towards Amanda.

Amanda ducked as the glass flew through the air. Water spilled in an almost perfect arc onto the ShellyServer. There was a sizzling sound as the lights on the side began flashing red.

As Ricardo's eyes darted from Drone to Tumble to the ShellyServer, Asha yanked her tablet from his hand. Ricardo tried to grab her, but she ducked away, dodged past Shelly and ran for the door.

"Come on!" Asha yelled at Tumble and Drone. "Chalo. Let's get out of here!"

| MY MISSIONS | MY TRAINING | MY INTEL |

The last thing you need on a mission is a grown-up to interrupt you with questions like:

> "What are you doing?"

> "How did you break into this super-secret evil lair?"

Grown-ups will believe anything if you sound confident enough. They don't question everything, unlike CSA agents.

What you need is a good cover story:

FAKE NAME

If they ask who you are, give them a fake name.

You can use one of our standard CSA cover names:

Sophie Deen, or Simon Deen, or Ali Bye, or Elle Owelle.

Pick a name, any name. Just not your name. Or Santa Claus.

FAKE JOB

Never tell anyone you're a secret agent, or it won't be secret. You can use one of our standard CSA cover jobs:

Chief Mischief Maker, or Happiness Ranger at Unicorn Box (a new tech start-up). Or you can make up a job, like astronaut, window cleaner or space-station window cleaner.

Chapter 13

...- .- .-. - ... / .- .-. . / .... . .-. -.-- / -.. ..
... - .-. .- .-.- - .. .- .--

13:20

Asha burst out into the corridor and glanced
around desperately. Shelly Inc seemed bigger
now they weren't in a ventilation shaft. Without
a map, Asha realized she had no idea how they
could escape. All she could see was a forest of
trees in large pots and signs for the ShellySlide.
She ran through their options. If they tried to
leave through the building's exits they would
be caught immediately. And they couldn't go
back through Shelly's office and into the
ventilation shaft.

The door flew open and Shelly and Ricardo sprinted towards them.

"Stop where you are, data thief!" Shelly marched towards Asha. She didn't sound so silky now. Her voice was gravelly with rage.

Ricardo was barking orders into his in-ear phone. "SECURITEEEYY! Double the guards on the perimeter of the building! Nobody under five foot tall, or made of metal, is allowed to leave. Yes, that's right, under five feet tall!"

"Did you see what I did to that panda-monkey?"

PUNCH
TODAY
IN THE
FACE!

Tumble held his right paw out for a high-five.

"High-fives later, Tumbs… I think I've got a plan!" said Asha. She reached into her backpack and pulled out her CSA selfie stick. "Hedy said that the selfie stick is encrypted with my fingerprints. And if anyone else tries to use it, the megafart will be activated. Tumble, give me that USB!" She grabbed the orange card and zipped it safely in her backpack. "I need you to take a selfie of us RIGHT NOW! And then we need to be ready to run – well, slide." Shelly and Ricardo were getting closer.

She passed the selfie stick to Tumble who attached his phone, pouted and hit the photo capture button at once, which gave a satisfying click. There was a brief flash of light, quickly followed by something far more deadly.

A vicious stench filled the air. "Asha, tell us the truth. Was that you? That's the worst fart ever!" Tumble wrinkled his nose.

MY MISSIONS   **MY TRAINING**   **MY INTEL**

This program scans the thumbprints of people who touch the selfie stick, so that it will only work for Asha. If anyone else uses it, it will release a megafart, which is very unpleasant.

When *the sensor is touched, read the thumbprint.* **If** *it's Asha, unlock the selfie stick and work normally.* **Otherwise***, it must not be Asha, so release the megafart using a function.*

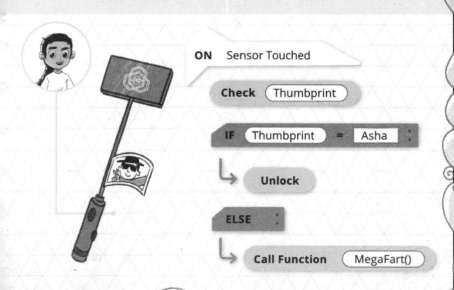

ON   Sensor Touched

Check (Thumbprint)

IF (Thumbprint) = (Asha) :

↳ **Unlock**

ELSE :

↳ **Call Function** (MegaFart())

What were the ingredients for such an effective fart smell? Asha would have to ask Hedy later.

Shelly and Ricardo were choking and coughing. Only Amanda seemed unaffected by the smell, but she couldn't keep up with Asha, Drone and Tumble as they sprinted towards the mouth of the ShellySlide.

They jumped into the dark opening. For a few moments, Asha forgot where she was. The slide was like a roller coaster, made up of big loops and windy bends.

"WOOOOOOOO! FASTER!"

Tumble yelled in delight as they hurtled round yet another corner.

Asha watched a circle of light grow bigger and then the three of them were flung out into the daylight. They skidded across a bouncy orange path onto a bright green lawn dotted with perfectly round bushes. Asha hurled herself behind one, panting.

She looked around. It was the same place that she had seen on television. Shelly's helicopter was waiting nearby, its propellers whirring.

"Shelly used that helicopter earlier," Asha whispered. "Maybe she's about to use it again."

Drone's eyes were as big as her screen. "We are NOT getting in that helicopter," she said. "I refer you to CSA Protocol 23.b. Hedy was very clear about Mission Shark Bytes. We need to take the DeepWater file to the ice-cream van, upload it to the CSA satellite network, and—"

But Asha wasn't listening. She was thinking about different protocols. CSA Protocols 1 and 2: Question Everything, Think For Yourself. It didn't mean sitting around and waiting for answers. It meant going out to find them yourself.

"If Shelly gets in that helicopter, we're

getting in there too! That's what spies do! We can sneak on board and follow her," said Asha. "Then, if we don't die or get caught, we'll find out exactly what she's up to. It's fine – we can upload the file to the network and give Hedy a full report on the way. Sorted!"

Drone hesitated. Her nannybot programming and even Asha's upgrades hadn't covered this situation. "OK," she replied eventually. "But only because I want you to save the Internet. And you must not take any FURTHER unnecessary risks, Asha!"

A moment later, Shelly and Ricardo came flying out of the ShellySlide. Shelly landed on both feet with a neat bounce, but Ricardo slid across the ground on his bum.

"Where are they?" he said, rising to his feet. "Have they escaped?"

"I'll pretend I didn't hear that, Ricardo." Shelly was speaking calmly again, but the hairs still stood up on Asha's neck. "I'll also pretend that my most important file hasn't just been stolen from under my feet and that my main server isn't currently in meltdown. I'm going to believe that you have the situation entirely under control and that those data-thieves are not going to leave here with a single byte of my intellectual property. Because I definitely don't need to think about firing you, or putting Code 3 into action, do I? You said that you'll take care of everything. So there's absolutely nothing for me to worry about."

"Absolutely! Totes! Completely! But should we delay our departure for SAP 21, just to be on the safe side? And I obvs don't want to use Code 3, Shells, but we might have to. The helicopter for Fishmouth is meant to depart in two minutes," Ricardo said.

"Mmmm..." replied Shelly, scrolling through her tablet. "No. SAP 21 is too urgent. We're going. But you will make this problem disappear, won't you Rickybae? You can manage Code 3 remotely and update me every five minutes, can't you? And I'll be flying that helicopter."

Asha turned to Tumble and Drone. "Did you

hear that? Shelly is going to somewhere called Fishmouth and that means we're all going too! Do you know where it is?"

"No, I don't." Drone hated admitting this. "I lost connection to ShellyNet 8 minutes and 23 seconds ago, while we were on the slide. I find it shocking that ShellyNet has such poor WiFi range. She should install some WiFi extenders on this roof and—"

"You don't know where Fishmouth is?" interrupted Tumble. "Do neither of you watch *Shelly by the Sea*?" He glanced at Drone's blank display and Asha's face. "It's where Shelly has her luxury beach resort and hangs out with her celeb frenemies," he added.

"The sea!" cried Asha, links quickly forming in her mind. "That MUST have something to do with the sharks! Drone, I'm going to Fishmouth. Are you guys coming?"

As Shelly and Ricardo climbed into the helicopter's cockpit, Asha and Tumble raced over and jumped in an open storage hatch near the tail. Drone hovered for a minute, muttering about health and safety regulations, before joining them.

Asha pulled the hatch closed, and the helicopter's engine began to judder beneath them. She felt a rush of excitement. This was what being a secret agent was all about.

Chapter 14

.... - . -. / - --- / .... . -.- .---

13:35

Asha, Tumble and Drone were huddled in the helicopter's storage compartment, squished between some odd-shaped ShellyNet boxes. It was cramped and uncomfortable but at least the noise completely drowned out their conversation. Shelly was piloting the helicopter, while Amanda curled up on a white cushion beside her. Ricardo was squished uncomfortably against the window, frantically typing on a tablet.

All sorts of thoughts were flying around Asha's mind. She probably wouldn't have to go to school now that she was part of a world-class spy network, and she definitely wouldn't have time for homework. Instead, she'd be busy taking video calls from agents all over the world and practising seeing in the dark.

But first, the Internet! Asha forced herself to focus on the mission. She needed to search Shelly's USB for the DeepWater file. "Let's see," she mumbled, as the helicopter bounced in the air. Her tablet pinged to life with a touch of her fingerprint and she inserted the USB. A line of letters appeared on the screen.

SHELLY INC

Enter password:

TSBHESB CSBOLSBOUSBR OFSB TSBHESB OCSBESBAN

"Hmm," said Asha. "It looks like some kind of cipher. Old school!"

"What if we ignore every SB in the sentence?" suggested Drone.

Asha squinted at the screen. "That works! It says … 'the colour of the ocean' … that's a hint. I bet the answer is blue."

"Blue?" Drone vibrated. "The ocean is actually TRANSPARENT." She flashed a line of text across her screen: *Humans, LOL.*

Asha ignored her, and typed in BLUE. ACCESS GRANTED flashed up on the screen.

Drone sighed. "Their system is wrong. Not me."

When the file on the USB opened, Asha typed DeepWater into the search bar. The tablet whirred as it searched through terabytes of data. Drone beeped, watching the loading wheel go round.

Suddenly, there was a loud noise from Asha's backpack. It was her CSA satellite phone. She pressed the receive button.

"Greetings, Agent Asha," said Hedy's computerized voice. "Have you located the file?

You have not yet returned to the ice-cream van and 66 minutes and 35 seconds have elapsed."

Asha looked at the spinning wheel on her screen. "Er … almost," she said. "But … good news … we've got a lead! We're following Shelly to Fishmouth. It's by the sea and we think that's where the next shark attack is going to be because—"

Hedy interrupted her. "When you get there, you will return home immediately. A CSA agent will now be dispatched to Fishmouth to investigate. Your mission was only to upload the file."

"But—" Asha spluttered.

"Agent Tyler will be at Fishmouth by the time you arrive. Tyler can use his oceanographic expertise to investigate exactly what Shelly is doing to the sharks. Your mission was clear, Agent Asha. Locate the file and upload it to the CSA."

The tablet let out a satisfied PING. The file had been located. Asha opened it and found dozens of smaller files. There was a SAP Map. It was so detailed that Asha couldn't really make sense of it.

"Drone?" asked Asha, putting her hand over the phone's speaker. "Can you abstract this map for me?"

"I have removed all the detail from the map apart from the location markers labelled SAP," Drone replied seconds later, flashing the map on her display.

"Look at the key, Drone! SAP stands for Shark Attack Points. The lines in the sea must be the Internet cables and the diamonds must be the locations where Shelly is luring the sharks," Asha whispered.

"Agent Asha?" Hedy's voice brought Asha back to the cramped compartment.

"Yes, sure. No worries. I'll upload the file as soon as I can." Before Hedy could say anything more, Asha hung up the phone and then froze.

Drone bleeped in alarm. "Why didn't you tell her that we've found the file?"

"Well ... it's totally not fair. Don't you want to know what's going on? Shouldn't we be thinking for ourselves? Also isn't it a BAD IDEA to NOT help Agent Tyler? We can't leave him on his own. He might get eaten by sharks! We'd have guilt-nightmares FOR EVER. We've got to get to the

bottom of this. And save the Internet." Asha's face got warm. She *did* feel guilty about lying to Hedy though and her words felt hollow.

And if Asha was completely honest with herself, she didn't know if hanging up on Hedy had been the right thing to do. This was the furthest she'd ever been from home without her parents or Anushka, and hiding in the dark was making her head hurt. Hedy had said there was now only one cable stopping the UK's entire Internet from going down. It wasn't just about Drone's lack of data, or Tumble's FaceSpace posts. What if ambulances didn't know where to go? Or people couldn't talk to their family in other countries? Or democracy was over? People could use ShellyNet, but only people who had lots of money – and even then Shelly Belly would control everything.

The CSA stood between the world and a real disaster. And right now, Asha and Agent Tyler – whoever he was – were the whole of the CSA.

Could they do it?

Asha took a deep breath. *The promises we make to*

ourselves are the most important ones, she thought to herself.

She was going to save the Internet. And a teenage trillionaire or a holographic plate of eggs wasn't going to get in the way. She took a deep breath. "We're going to help Agent Tyler, stop Shelly and get back to the ice-cream van without Hedy knowing anything about it."

Drone gave a hum of disapproval. "And your plan, Asha?"

"I've got a few strategies," replied Asha.

"You are using a long word like 'strategies' to hide the fact you don't have a plan, aren't you?" said Drone.

"Maybe," said Asha.

"In that case, the best approach would be to use decomposition," said Drone.

"Decomposition!" said Tumble. "I told you that zombies were involved!"

Asha and Drone both giggled.

"Not exactly, Tumble. Decomposition is a way of breaking down big problems into smaller parts and tackling them one at a time," Drone explained.

"Good idea, Drone. It's a great way to solve problems," said Asha. She dug out her notebook from her backpack and wrote down each part of the problem. There were quite a few stages.

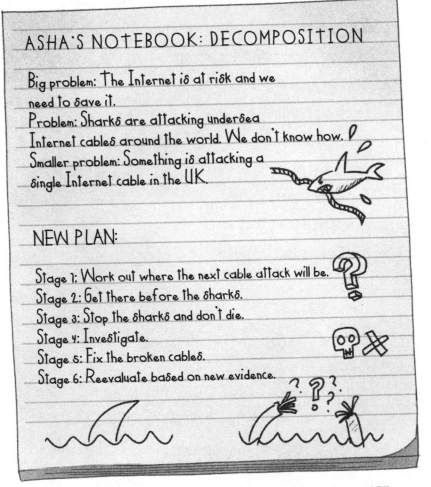

ASHA'S NOTEBOOK: DECOMPOSITION

Big problem: The Internet is at risk and we need to save it.
Problem: Sharks are attacking undersea Internet cables around the world. We don't know how.
Smaller problem: Something is attacking a single Internet cable in the UK.

NEW PLAN:

Stage 1: Work out where the next cable attack will be.
Stage 2: Get there before the sharks.
Stage 3: Stop the sharks and don't die.
Stage 4: Investigate.
Stage 5: Fix the broken cables.
Stage 6: Reevaluate based on new evidence.

Stage 1 was sorted. They'd already found the map of Shark Attack Points. Stage 2 was harder because they'd need to get out to sea. Hopefully they'd be able to find a boat at the seaside. That's where boats lived. Stage 3 was probably the most problematic. It was only really worth worrying about 4, 5 and 6 if they got past it.

Twenty-three minutes later, they had a lot of ideas for stopping the sharks. Asha's first thought was to use underwater radios to transmit loud noises. Maybe she could play one of Anushka's latest music tracks.

But, as Drone pointed out, they didn't have any radios. Then Asha wondered if they could paint the cables pink and green, so they looked like venomous snakes. But

SNAKES?

they didn't have any scuba-diving gear, they didn't know how to scuba-dive, paint wouldn't work underwater and sharks didn't know about snakes.

"These plans are smart!" Tumble was impressed. "We just don't have any of the right equipment."

But what about Agent Tyler? Asha thought to herself. He'd have hi-tech shark stuff with him, right? They needed to find him as soon as they arrived in Fishmouth.

Eventually the helicopter began to descend. The engine fell silent as it touched down.

Asha could hear Shelly and Ricardo speaking in muffled voices. What were they talking about? She couldn't make it out. For a moment, her heart began to race as the voices got louder. It sounded as though they were right outside the hatch to the storage compartment. But then, just like that, the voices got quieter again.

"Let's go," said Asha.

She pulled open the hatch and peeked outside. The coast was clear. She jumped down and made a run for it, with Tumble and Drone close behind.

Chapter 15

.... --- .... --- --- ... .. .- -- ... / .-. ... .

16:03

Fishmouth was a classic seaside town. Candy floss, deckchairs, plastic buckets and spades.

Asha, Tumble and Drone tried to run down the crowded promenade, but it was hard work weaving in and out of all the holidaymakers enjoying a sunny Saturday. Outside each fish and chip shop, there were long queues of angry people trying to pay. Cashiers in hairnets tried desperately to explain that their tills wouldn't work without the Internet.

Drone buzzed worriedly around Asha's head.

"This plan is inefficient," she said. "Based on the size of the town, I calculate that there are approximately 2,000 people in a one-kilometre radius. We only have a 4 per cent chance of locating Agent Tyler."

But as Asha was scanning the crowd, her eyes narrowed.

A moment later, she gasped. "There! Look!" Tumble and Drone stopped and followed Asha's finger.

"The Fishy Business Café?" asked Tumble doubtfully.

"Good thinking," said Drone. "My records show that it has been 5 hours and 34 minutes since your last full meal. You require food, Asha. You know that you get hangry."

"No, Drone, I'm fine," cried Asha impatiently. "I've got raisins if I get desperate. Look! Do you see that glint of light?"

At one end of the beach was a boy wearing sunglasses propped on his forehead. He was standing beside a long wooden jetty which stretched out to the sea. He looked slightly older than Asha, and had a very large backpack swinging at his side. Attached to the backpack was an odd, shiny item, twinkling in the afternoon sun.

Drone whirred in excitement as her camera zoomed in. "It's a holograph!"

"Yep," said Asha triumphantly. "And I bet it's exactly the same logo as the one that we found in the library. He's CSA! That must be Agent Tyler."

They hurried towards the boy, passing another long line of people waiting at a row of cash machines. Every screen was flashing the same message: ERROR: NO INTERNET CONNECTION.

Asha tried to put other people's problems out of her mind. Agent Tyler was her priority. As she got closer, she saw that he was frowning at his phone, clearly waiting for something – or someone.

"Agent Tyler?" asked Asha. Finally she was

meeting a real-life secret agent! She'd never met one before. Apart from herself, of course. As of this morning, anyway. The boy looked up, his face surprised.

"Who are you?" He spoke with an American accent.

"I'm Agent Asha. I'm also with the CSA and I'm trying to stop Shelly Belly," Asha replied. "I mean, I just woke up, got the email link to the vegetable website, then there was that librarian with the otter earrings, a talking plate of eggs, a massive slide, a helicopter, and THEN—"

"Are you the ocean expert?" Drone asked, interrupting Asha.

Tyler smiled at Asha before looking to Drone and nodding. "Yep. I could swim before I could crawl. The CSA got in touch after I organized a big seaweed planting effort in my state." Asha opened her mouth, but Tyler was ahead of her. "The thing about seaweed farms is that they help to absorb CO_2 and increase bio-productivity. I'm not just ... really into seaweed."

Asha could hardly contain her excitement. Here was someone else who liked roping people into experiments as much as she did! What question should she ask first? Do sharks have a soul? How many sharks are there in the ocean? How do they talk to each other? How fast can they swim?

"Hedy briefed me on the mission," continued Tyler. "I'm to review the data in the DeepWater file – which Hedy says you are to upload immediately – and confirm if Shelly Belly is using sharks to bite through Internet cables."

Asha looked at Tumble and Drone. "Um, I've already had a quick look at the file. Shelly is definitely using sharks."

"Whoa, OK," said Tyler. "But we still don't know if she is luring the sharks to the cables or if she has trained them to attack them. I need to gather more data. My plan is to release some tasty shark food – we call it chum – it's a lot tastier than fibre-optic Internet cables. Hopefully, that will bring the sharks to the surface. From there, I'll be able to investigate what Shelly has done to them and then hopefully we can stop them."

Tyler unzipped his backpack and pulled out a spiral-bound notebook. It was sprinkled with sand and had a strong fishy smell. Asha tried not to wrinkle up her nose.

"A notebook?" Asha was surprised. "Won't the pages get wet?"

Tyler chuckled. "It's CSA kit. The pages are totally waterproof. I can use this notepad at the bottom of the sea. Now, let me show you my plan…"

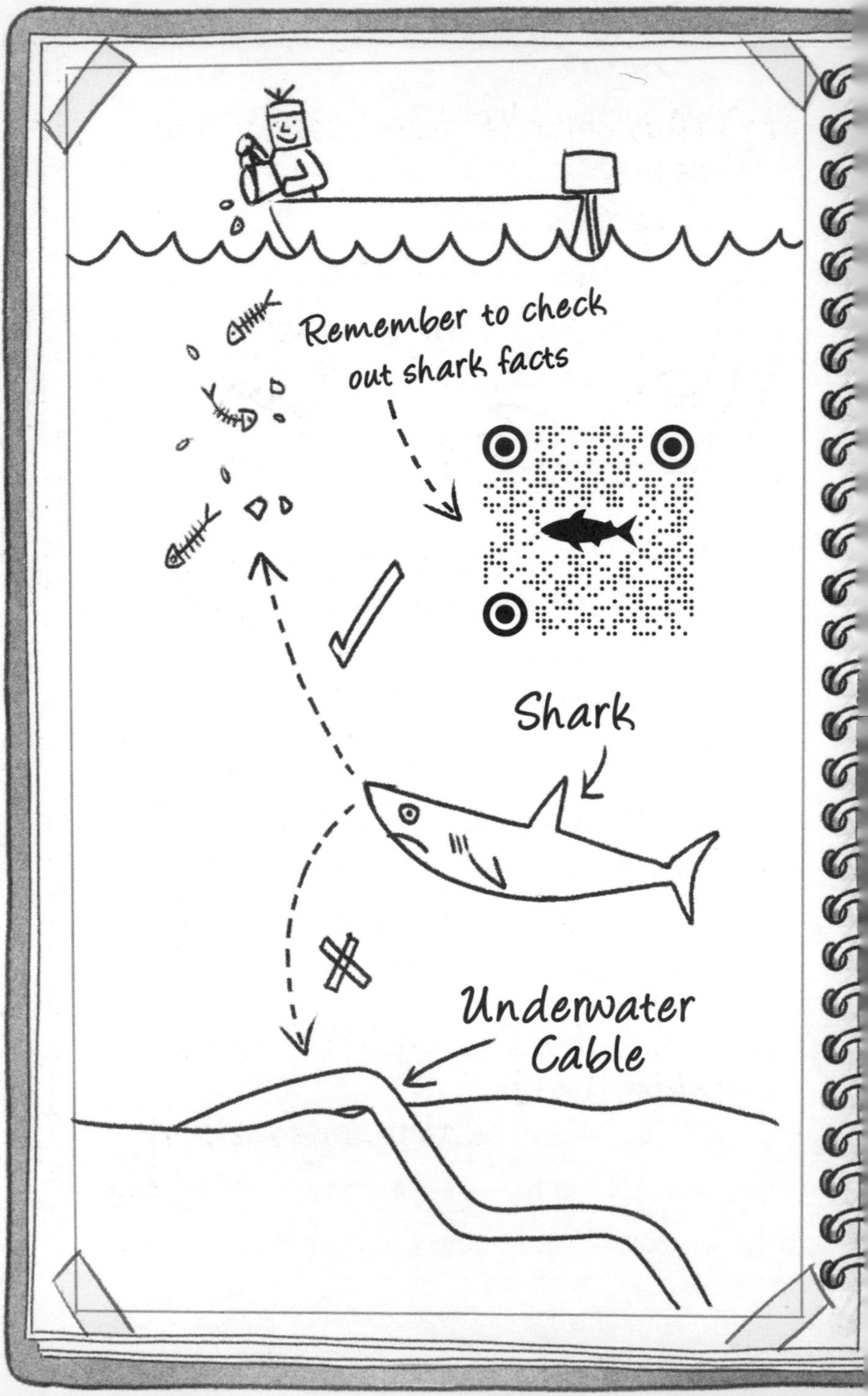

Remember to check out shark facts

Shark

Underwater Cable

① Molecules of chum dissolve into seawater.

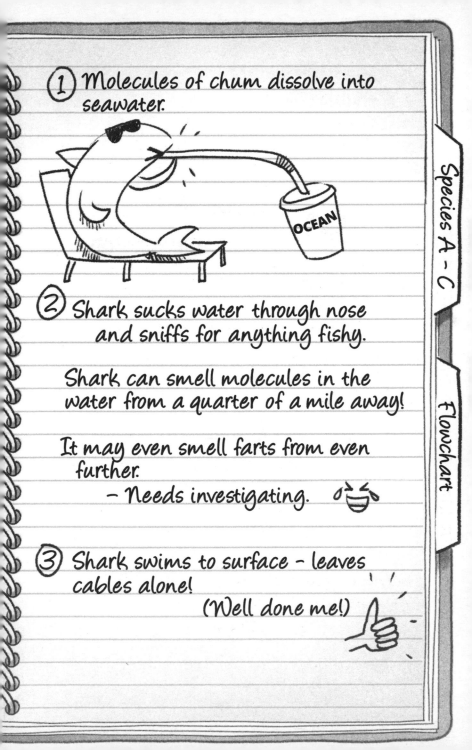

② Shark sucks water through nose and sniffs for anything fishy.

Shark can smell molecules in the water from a quarter of a mile away!

It may even smell farts from even further.
— Needs investigating.

③ Shark swims to surface — leaves cables alone!
(Well done me!)

Asha nodded. She liked Tyler's plan.

"So, what are we dealing with here?" Tyler asked. "I figured I'd just have the DeepWater file to go on, but, hey, if Hedy's assigned you to work with me, then that's cool too."

Asha hesitated as she took out her tablet. "I mean, she didn't *exactly* assign me to work with you," she said quietly.

Tyler was so impressed by Drone that he didn't seem to hear Asha's mumbling. "Wow, this is one seriously upgraded nannybot." He admired her propellers. "Are you waterproof? I could use you to take photos when I'm surfing." Tyler turned to look at Tumble. "And who is this little cutie. Is it a—?"

"Tyler," said Asha impatiently. She had opened the file and found a photo of a severed cable. "I think these are the sharks that Shelly is using. Do you recognize this kind of bite mark?"

Tyler took the screen and looked over it carefully. A frown appeared on his face as he stared at the picture. "Whoa. This doesn't look like any species I've seen before. And I've certainly not heard of anything like this in these waters. Let me check my flowcharts." Tyler narrowed his eyes. "I can't find a match. Judging by the shape of the bite mark and the size and the position of the holes made by the teeth … well, I've never seen a shark like this before."

"So she's using an undiscovered species?" asked Asha.

"I don't know." Tyler looked down at his flowcharts again. "I'd be surprised if she'd found a new species, but who knows.

Round and deep like they're from an ice-cream scoop?

When you look closer, kind of scratchy with rows of cuts inside each bite?

COOKIE CUTTER SHARK?

yes

No, it's like a rabbit has been chewing on a carrot

The scratches are shallow and bumpy

HORN SHARK?

The scratches are twisted and deep

FRILLED SHARK?

GHOST SHARK?

Stranger things have happened. Around six thousand new ocean species are discovered every year."

"The thing I don't understand is why Shelly is in Fishmouth," Asha said. "If she's trained the sharks, why does she need to be here?" Asha pushed her chin up. "But yeah, between the two of us, we can probably figure this out..." Asha didn't feel sure at all.

Tyler smiled. "We sure can. I've requested a CSA boat, and once it arrives then—"

He was interrupted by Drone swooping down between him and Asha. Her lights were flashing a disco level of danger as she flew towards the jetty.

"Warning! There is no time to wait for a CSA vessel!" she cried.

A black speedboat was setting out to sea in the distance. A teenage girl with white hair was sitting beside the driver with a distinctive topknot.

It was Shelly.

Chapter 16

.-- . -- . -- -.-. . .-- / .-. .-. --- - --- -.-. ---

-.-. / .-. .. .-. - -.-- / ... . .-. . -..

16:14

Tyler didn't know what to do. "Well ... erm ... as soon as the CSA boat gets here we should report back and then foll—"

"We've got zero time to waste," said Asha. "Shelly's heading to the SAP RIGHT NOW. Like, literally. Something important must be happening. Maybe she's attacking the final cable. We need to get out there, fast!"

"Asha, you are breaking CSA protocol. We should call Hedy and—"

"We don't have time. Come on, Tyler. Let's go!"

"Fine," said Tyler, shrugging. "If you think Hedy won't mind."

Asha ran down the jetty towards a row of moorings. A boat was bobbing on the waves. It was small, but it looked quite new and its engine gleamed in the sun.

Perfect.

Asha and Tyler crept down the jetty. They jumped into the boat, trying not to attract attention. It swayed underneath them.

"Stay low," Asha whispered. "I just need to figure out how to start the engine. And then how to drive it."

"Don't worry," replied Tyler, a dimple appearing on his left cheek. "I can drive this boat – and almost any boat." The dimple disappeared. "But it looks like the engine is password protected."

"Ah, that won't be a problem," replied Asha, flexing her fingers. "I can hack that in minutes."

"I can do it in seconds," said Drone.

DRONE VS ASHA

Skill: brute force hack (tries every possible number and letter combination until one works). Problem solving without influence of human emotion. Doesn't need to go to the toilet.

Skill: critical thinking (finding patterns, spotting connections, analysing information). Advance humour, imagination, empathy. Does need to go to the toilet.

Brute force hack engaged. Calculating every possible combination.

Critical thinking activated. What do I know about the owner? Like, I don't know if they have a dog, but I do know they have a boat.

BOAT. Dinghy1. DinghyDingy. DingDong.

Dinghy-a-ling. NotAYacht. BoatyBoat. BoatsForever.

Uh... Drone...?

Do not interrupt, tiny hamster.

Look what I found.

Boat pass: SEAWATER (don't forget)

Ohhhhh!

Asha typed in the password, and the screen flashed green with a high-pitched ping.

There was a GPS option, and Asha entered the coordinates of the Shark Attack Points she'd found in Shelly's file. Then she pulled on a life jacket and turned back to Tyler, holding out one for him.

His eyebrows were raised as he put it on. "How often do you three hack into things?" he asked. "Or steal boats? Usually the CSA doesn't let us."

"We never normally break the law. Instead, we use simulated environments. I win most of the time," Drone beeped. She loved talking about security. "But that password was human-level basic. I would suggest that—"

"HEY!" A shout pierced the air. A woman was running towards them down the jetty.

"I don't think she's in the mood for your password advice," Asha said to Drone.

Drone started to panic. "There is a 72 per cent chance that the owner of the boat will catch us in less than 58 seconds and that is very problematic, as I am 100 per cent sure that stealing a boat is illegal."

"Thanks for the update." Asha bit the inside of her cheeks. "Can we go now, Tyler?"

"Just … one … second…" Tyler was hunched over the controls of the boat, frantically pressing buttons and flicking switches.

"Don't worry," said Tumble. "I can protect us!" He adopted a power stance on the steering wheel, overbalanced, and fell into the bottom of the boat. Drone hovered for a moment before flying down to join him.

The motor roared into life.

"Sorry! We're not pirates! Triple promise! We'll bring your boat back soon," Asha yelled back to the confused owner. "Just as soon as we've saved the Internet."

Chapter 17

... --- -- · - .... .. -. --- / .. ... / ...·- .. ...
.... -.--

16:26

Asha felt like her heart was about to
burst. With Tyler at the helm, the boat
was tearing through the water like scissors
through wrapping paper. This was more
like it: everything had become 300 per cent
more spy. They were heading at top speed
towards dangerous sharks.

"Don't tell Hedy I said this, but stealing
a boat isn't ... un-fun." Tyler had to shout
the words over the roar of the wind.

"Totally!" said Asha, with a wide smile. But then a flash of guilt passed through her mind. She'd never stolen anything before. But people's lives depended on them stopping Shelly from destroying the final cable. Was it OK to do something wrong in order to do something right? She made a mental note to check with Nana-Ji and to ask Drone to double-check the CSA protocols about stealing and borrowing … but not until they'd completed the mission.

Tumble stood at the front of the boat, shouting warnings to the waves. "Go Team CSA!" he yelled at the top of his voice, preparing to snap a boat-selfie. Drone hummed in disapproval.

"Tyler," Drone said, flitting about in the air, "please advise on your course of action."

"We should dump the chum two hundred metres from the first SAP," Tyler replied. "That will lure the sharks away from the cable and to the surface. Then we can see what Shelly has done to them!"

Tumble jumped onto the flat area at the very front of the boat, struggling to keep his balance. "Those sharks are going to wish they'd never learnt to swim!"

Asha reached over to grab him so he didn't fall overboard. Tyler stood at the controls, looking preoccupied.

"What are you thinking about?" asked Asha.

Tyler sighed. "I don't know. It's just ... I'd be really impressed if Shelly had managed to train a shark. They are pretty independent and also they shouldn't be anywhere near Fishmouth. The sea here is really cold. Most big breeds of shark like things a little bit warmer … and I do too." He pulled down the sleeves of his hoodie.

Asha took a moment to consider what he was saying. Why were they so certain it was a shark? "Tyler, if I remember right, there are two things that connect the cables to the sharks: the ripped cables and that diver, Kim Lau, her footage from the seabed. In the report Hedy played, she was certain she'd seen a shark. Everything else has come from Shelly."

"What are you suggesting, Asha? That she isn't using sharks after all?"

"I don't know. But maybe we should be asking more questions, rather than just accepting what we've been told." She shut her eyes and tried to concentrate on the data she had. What could damage the cables so deep underwater? Submarines? A giant octopus? Explosives? Could you even explode things underwater? The cables had bite marks on them, so it surely had to be a creature. Asha's mind drifted to Amanda, Shelly's infamous pet (half monkey, half panda) and a thought struck her; if Shelly would mess with DNA just to make a pet, what was stopping her from creating a new species of cable-munching shark altogether?!

Asha opened her eyes again. The solution still didn't feel quite right to her.

"Whatever it is, we'll find out soon." Tyler glanced at the map. "We're almost there."

Tyler cut the motor and Asha squinted towards Shelly's boat in the distance. They'd stopped too. It looked as though they were bent over the sides, watching a spot in the water.

It was shark time.

Tyler opened his backpack and tipped a foul-smelling mixture of fish and oil over the side.

"See ya later, buddy," he murmured. "Or as you'd say in England – goodbye, old chum! We should be seeing some hungry sharks very soon."

"As long as they aren't hangry," said Drone.

They all looked over the side of the boat,

watching the chum disappear beneath the waves. They strained their eyes, waiting to see a fin.

Nothing. Not so much as a kipper.

"That's weird," Tyler said after a while. "That mixture of chum always works."

"Maybe Shelly is doing something to them," said Asha. "Drone, can you fly over to Shelly's boat and see if you can spot any sharks?"

"But don't sharks eat robots?" Drone sounded

anxious. "How high can they jump?" Her internal fan whirred. "I don't have access to the relevant safety protocols right now. I can't even find the video archive from BigSharkFan400. I do not have enough information to decide on a correct course of action. ERROR!"

"Drone, don't worry. You'll be fine – the sharks won't be interested in you," said Asha, trying to appear confident. It was strange to hear Drone sound so unsure.

Drone hesitated. "As I cannot use the Internet to check the facts, I have no option but to follow your instructions, Asha." Her propellers whirred as she took off from the side of the boat and flew out across the water.

Asha watched her go. Drone would be fine … right? She was a tiny metal robot, not a tasty tuna or a surfer. But then again, neither were the cables.

Asha's insides were tossing and turning, just like the sea. Wave after wave rocked the boat. As Drone became a dot in the sky, Asha's chest started to tighten. She'd been ignoring Drone's warnings all day, but Drone had been right every time. Getting herself into trouble was one thing, but sending a 3 kilogram drone off on her own to deal with a 1,000 kilogram shark was another matter.

What if she got hurt?

"Tyler, stop!" Asha felt panic rising in her. "I want to go after Drone."

Tyler went to move the steering wheel, shading his eyes against the sky.

"Hang on, Asha. I think she's coming back!"

They watched as Drone hurtled towards them, barely skimming the waves.

"SELACHIMORPHA! SELACHIMORPHA!" They heard Drone's alarm sounding. Just beneath her, a fin was slicing through the water.

"That's the biggest dorsal fin I've ever seen!" said Tyler, eyes locked on it.

"Faster, Drone, faster!" Asha yelled.

The dark shape began to rise out of the water. A huge pair of open jaws with rows of razor-sharp teeth appeared above the waves, lunging for Drone.

"Shark!" cried Tumble.

Transfixed by the size of the beast, Asha's mouth fell open. The shark had two blue lights blinking where its eyes should be.

Hedy had been wrong.

"That's not a shark!" cried Tyler.

"No," said Asha. "IT'S A ROBOT!"

Chapter 18

.---- --- .. -. / ... ...

16:34

The shark's snapping jaws caught Drone's wing. It tore through the metal as though it was butter, and her wires spilled out. Drone wobbled in the air, trying to keep her balance.

The shark hit the water. It lay on the surface for a moment, before sinking out of sight.

"Drone!" shrieked Asha. "We're coming! Fly as high as you can! Just don't get wet!"

The shark exploded from the water again, lunging towards Drone with gaping jaws. Drone tried to hover out of its reach, but her damaged wing made it hard for her to stay in the air.

Tumble jumped onto the side of the boat, clutching a bright red first-aid kit that was about four times his size.

"Leave her alone!" he shouted, launching the first-aid kit into the air. The box flew through the air and landed in the shark's open mouth. Plasters flew everywhere, but the box temporarily wedged the snapping jaws open and the shark sank out of sight.

Drone crash-landed into the boat. She was vibrating with fear and loops of cable were dangling from her side. Asha knelt down beside her, checking the extent of the damage. To her relief, her main circuits were still intact. "I should never ever have sent you off like that," Asha said, trying to hold back tears. "I'm so sorry."

Drone's pixel-eyes glowed gold with warmth. Asha was about to say more, when the boat was hit by a huge wave. She grabbed hold of the side as the boat swayed beneath her.

The shark was rising out of the waves right next to their boat.

"We need to get out of here," Tyler shouted.

Asha gave Drone to Tumble, who ran his paws over her damaged wing, a look of worry on his face and the sad emoji flashing repeatedly on his display.

"How fast can this thing go?" she yelled back at Tyler. Anger and fear surged inside her. Taking the Internet down was one thing, but hurting Drone was another thing entirely. Asha was going to stop Shelly, and she was going to stop her now.

"This fast," responded Tyler, as the engine roared and he sent the boat skimming across the water.

The wind whipped Asha's hair, and for a second she forgot about the fact she might be about to die in a robot-shark race. She could feel the adrenaline running through her.

But when she looked behind her, her fear returned. They were going at full throttle, but the shark was easily matching their speed. It raced through the waves, its electronic eyes devoid of any expression. *Will it hurt to get eaten by a robot?* Asha wondered, as the shark drew level with the back of the boat.

"Leave the squad alone," Tumble yelled. He had managed to grab the end of an emergency oar in his tiny paws and was jabbing it at the shark.

CHOMP!

Tumble was left holding a splinter.

The chance of being shark dinner was increasing

with every second. With Tyler steering, Asha did what she did best.

Concentrate, Asha told herself. *Think*.

Then it hit her: robots don't think. They just follow the instructions in their programming. This shark was terrifying, but it was just a robot. It was following instructions in its code. Shelly must have invented it and then programmed it to destroy the cables.

So why was it attacking their boat and not the cable? A human must have changed the robot's code. Someone must be reprogramming the shark right now.

Asha looked up and saw Shelly's boat was just behind the shark. She was hunched over a tablet, while Ricardo steered the boat. *Of course,* Asha thought. Shelly wasn't going to let anything get in the way of her plan.

But it looked as though Shelly needed to be close to the shark to program it. Why? Wait ... if she was using a tablet, and there was no Internet, she had to be using Bluetooth, like the robot butterfly at Shelly Inc. Of course! Bluetooth signal had a maximum range of one hundred metres! And that wasn't its only weakness...

"ICANHACKTHESHARK!" Asha yelled. She was so excited that her words rolled into one.

"You can smack the fart?" Tyler was confused.

"I CAN HACK THE SHARK," Asha tried again.

"Now we're talking!" Tyler grinned.

"Just keep us within one hundred metres of it," said Asha. "We need to stay in range."

"That won't be a problem." Tyler glanced over his shoulder, where the shark was still right on their tail, surging through the waves.

The boat bucked and lurched, but Asha's hands were steady, as she pulled her tablet from her backpack and turned on Bluetooth. The tablet scanned for all the devices in range. There was only one: SHELLYJAWS. Asha connected to the shark's Bluetooth signal, but the robot was password protected. If she couldn't crack the password, she wouldn't be able to access its programming. She looked down at Drone lying in the bottom of the boat. This time she wouldn't have Drone's help.

She thought back to the password that they'd seen on the desk in Shelly's office. It felt like a lifetime ago, but she could still remember it: #il0vedeadlin3s. Was the shark's password something similar? #il0vesharks. Nope, that didn't work. #il0vewat3r. Yes! She was in! Drone was right that humans could be very stupid. Shelly was one of the best coders in the world, but she really needed to work on her passwords.

Next, Asha needed to reprogram the shark. *It's not even a real shark*, Asha kept telling herself, *just a robot*. She could control it.

There was a loud clank as the shark snapped at the boat, missing their engine by inches. Between those savage metal jaws, it would be boat-flavoured ice cream.

"Asha?" Tyler cleared his throat. "Is there any chance you could … speed up with whatever you're doing?"

Asha didn't reply. She frantically typed on her tablet. The motor was roaring louder than ever and the sea was surging and slapping at the sides of the boat as they bounced through the waves.

A shadow fell across her screen.

She looked up to see that the shark had thrust itself almost completely out of the water. Its jaws were level with the back of the boat, open and ready to snap.

Tumble froze into his toy pose. Tyler closed his eyes and covered his face.

One more second, and they would be fish food.

But Asha didn't need one more second. With beads of sweat on her upper lip and eyes locked on the screen, she closed the final line of code, and pressed the run symbol. She held her breath.

ON Update

IF Boat Proximity ≤ 1m

Turn Left 90°

ELSE

Wave Fin

The shark twisted in mid-air, missing the boat by a matter of inches and landing in the water with a gigantic splash.

"YESSSSSSS!" said Asha triumphantly.

The shark was lying still in the water, gently waving its top fin as if it was dancing to music no one else could hear. Tyler slowed the boat down, and circled it back towards the shark. Tumble started jumping up and down, pumping his fist.

"What did you do?" asked Tyler, his eyes wide.

Asha's cheeks were tingling. "It had a set of prearranged instructions. All I had to do was get inside and change them. It was programmed to swim after our boat. I created a loop instead."

"A loop?" Tyler tilted his head.

"It's when your code tells a computer to do something, and then once it's done it, to go back to the start and do it all over again. And if it's a forever loop, it will keep going around and around the loop forever – or until an event happens to change it. Here, have a look."

Asha leaned forward so that Tyler could see her

tablet screen. She rearranged the blocks of code with a flick of her finger.

The shark flipped over and began doing a gentle backstroke alongside the boat. Tyler laughed in amazement.

"We're a pretty good team, Asha." He grinned at her. "I steer the boat and you steer the sharks!"

"Asha?" Drone was still lying in the bottom of the boat. "I'm… I feel…" Her voice glitched a little and went into rhyming mode. "There once was a robot named Drone, more useful than any smartphone. Then she went in the water, a shark nearly caught her, now her circuits have somewhat been blown..."

Asha had been so distracted by the shark that she'd forgotten to check up on Drone. "Let me take a look at you," she said, kneeling down beside the nannybot and reaching for the What-A-Bottle multitool.

But as Asha's knees hit the bottom of the boat, a massive wave washed over the side, soaking them all.

The black speedboat was right beside them. Shelly was standing up, looking furiously at her tablet.

"You again," she snarled, as she locked eyes with Asha.

Chapter 19

-.-. .... . -.-. --- / - .... . / -... .- -.-. --- / ---
.... / - .... . / -... --- --- ---

16:39

"I'm going to say this once!" shouted Shelly. "So
make sure your tiny, tiny ears can hear me. GET.
AWAY. FROM. MY. SHARK!"

"It's not your shark any more!" Asha yelled back.
"I've hacked it!"

"Yeah, and it doesn't matter what size her ears
are," Tumble added. "It's the size of her hearing that
counts."

Ricardo spun the speedboat round and angled
it towards Asha's boat. From the noise of Ricardo's
revving, Shelly's engine was far more powerful

than theirs. It would tear straight through their little boat. She quickly reached for her tablet and programmed the shark to swim between the two boats.

Shelly's boat powered towards the shark. They were going to collide.

At the last moment, Ricardo steered the speedboat away from the robot. But it took a while for the big boat to change its course.

That's our advantage, Asha thought. *We may be small, but we can move fast.*

An unfamiliar line of code scrolled up her tablet screen. Shelly had taken over the Bluetooth!

```
ON   Update
   WHILE   InWater   =   True
      Swim   Forwards
         IF   Boat   Proximity $   1m
            Bite
   RETURN to loop start
```

Panic swept over Asha as the shark changed direction, paused for two seconds, and then swam straight for their boat's engine, its mouth wide open.

"Tyler, do something!"

Tyler swerved hard, moving the boat just beyond the shark's jaws. They closed with a crunch of metal, just missing the engine.

"That was way too close," Tyler gasped.

Asha took a deep breath. Shelly was the most famous coder in the world. She'd built complex machines, autonomous AI and … robot sharks. But Asha was the most stubborn person in the world. Once she set her mind on something, there was no stopping her. She was going to fight Shelly for control of the shark and she was going to win.

Probably.

Hopefully.

Asha looked back at her tablet. If she could program the shark to turn 360 degrees in a forever loop, then it'd be stuck spinning on the spot. She started tapping on her tablet.

Tumble was jumping around the deck, karate-chopping the air. "If that shark comes near us again, I'll give it a taste of steel."

"OK," whispered Asha to herself, barely moving her lips as she sent her code to the shark's Bluetooth receiver. "I think I've done it."

The shark began to spin around on the spot.

Tumble launched himself from the side of the boat onto its back. "Jaws, meet Paws! No one treats my friend Drone like that! It's #TimeForT!"

"Wait, Tumble, stop! What are you doing? You're not waterproof," said Asha. "Hold this while I grab him." She shoved her tablet into Tyler's hands.

ON Update

WHILE This = True

Turn Right 360°

RETURN to loop start

Tyler's eyes widened. "My coding isn't—"

But Asha wasn't listening. She was already at the side of the boat, reaching for Tumble. The shark was spinning so fast that Tumble was an orange blur on its dark back. It was a good thing robots couldn't get dizzy. He was only just managing to cling on to the metal body. "Tyler! Can't you get us any closer?" screamed Asha.

"On it!" Tyler shouted back, bringing the boat alongside the shark. Asha reached out, just as Tumble whizzed past her. She couldn't quite grab him.

"I'm actually dying!" Tumble yelled.

"Asha," said Tyler, staring at the tablet in his hand. "I think Shelly is trying to get control again."

"Hold on!"

Asha leaned out of the boat and managed to grab Tumble with the tips of her fingers. She felt a rush of relief as she dropped Tumble in the boat, and turned back to take the tablet from Tyler.

But it was too late. Shelly's code had already flashed up.

"Ready for my tooth torpedo?" shouted Shelly.

The boat rocked back and forth, as the shark swam beneath them.

"What's happening, Asha?" asked Tumble.

"Asha," pleaded Tyler. "I think the shark is underneath us. If it bites through the bottom of the boat, that's it. You need to hurry. You've got this. Come on, go, go go!"

"I can't keep up with her coding," cried Asha. "She's too good. Tyler, we need to pair program, like, NOW now, and code at the same time. We'll have a better chance of not-dying if we do this together. You need to check that I'm not making any mistakes in my code."

Tyler's eyes narrowed. "I've got a better idea."

He reached into his backpack and pulled out a small bag of chum. Could Asha see a fish eye in there? Before she had time to take a closer look, Tyler had launched the bag through the air.

The bag exploded on Shelly's head like a fishy grenade. Fish guts splattered down her shoulders, and onto her tablet. She screamed.

Ricardo tried to brush the fish guts out of her eyes, but Shelly wasn't having any of it.

"Where were you?" Shelly spat out a glob of chum. "You're contractually obliged to take bullets for me."

"My contract doesn't mention fish guts, otherwise I totes would have," Ricardo whined.

"Really?" asked Shelly, furiously. "I'm pretty sure that sub-clause 6.1 says exactly that. "Maybe you need to take another compulsory weekend of training, Ricky, and remind yourself how to be you, but better."

The fishy distraction was all that Asha needed. She finished her code, held her breath and pressed run. Bluetooth sent the data to the shark's receiver in less than a second.

If this worked, then it would be game over for Shelly.

The shark burst out of the water and began swimming away from the two boats and out to sea as fast as it possibly could.

"What did you do?" yelled Shelly, waving her tablet.

"What did you do?" asked Tyler, amazed.

ON Update

WHILE This = True :

Swim Forward Speed = 30mph

RETURN to loop start

"I set the shark to move forward, at ten times its normal speed, in a forever loop." Asha grinned, as the pointed fin disappeared over the horizon. "Bluetooth connections only work over limited distances, so Shelly can't reprogram the shark unless she catches up with it."

"FOLLOW THAT SHARK," yelled Shelly. "I'm going to get you for this!" she said, turning to look at Asha.

Ricardo raced after the shark, but it was already too late. With every second, it was getting further out of range. The shark would be swimming until Shelly caught it or its batteries ran out.

The four of them were safe and so was the Internet cable.

"Boom, mission complete," said Tyler. "Let's
get back to dry land and report in to Hedy. She'll
know what to do next." Asha high-fived Tyler then
scooped Tumble up into a hug. Drone was still
lying at the bottom of the boat, but she managed a
beep of relief, which sounded a little like a hiccup.
Team CSA had saved the day.

Chapter 20

--- --- / - --- / ---- ... .- / -.. --- - / .--- --- ...
....

17:52

Asha had never seen a dessert look angry before, but somehow an ice-cream-shaped Hedy was managing it. Her holographic wafer wobbled menacingly.

The CSA ice-cream van had been waiting for them by the jetty in Fishmouth. As soon as Asha had clambered into the back, Hedy had appeared and begun her debrief.

"You disobeyed Protocol 10 to abandon missions when instructed to," she said. "This is inexcusable."

"But Protocol 2 is to think for yourself,"

protested Asha and then had to stop to burp. She'd found some ice cream in the CSA van and having not had a proper meal since breakfast, she'd eaten rather a lot. "Also it doesn't matter exactly what I did, does it? The important thing is that we succeeded!"

Asha and Tyler had come back to shore buzzing after their showdown with Shelly. The boat had been returned to its owner and Tyler was staying in Fishmouth to help Kim Lau, the engineer who had first seen the sharks. They were going to repair the damaged cables and add some further shark-proofing so nothing like this could happen again with sharks – robotic or otherwise. As far as Asha was concerned, Mission Shark Bytes had been a success.

Apart from what had happened to Drone. Asha laid her hand on the robot, who was lying between her and a very protective Tumble. Thankfully, there was no major harm and Drone just needed a couple of wires and a panel replacing. She was powered down until Asha could fix her.

"Success is relative. Your actions have consequences. Once Shelly knew her file had been stolen, she tried to access government intelligence across the world to reclaim  her data. We've had to deal with multiple breaches. Protocol 2 is very important," said ice-cream-Hedy, interrupting Asha's thoughts. "But I must still weigh up your actions in full. How you achieve your objective is as significant as the objective itself."

"But nothing went wrong," said Asha. "Not really, anyway."

"Breaking Protocol 10 could have led to the failure of the overall mission, not its success," continued Hedy. "You are part of something bigger than just yourself, Asha Joshi. Last week, an agent refused to abort her mission. She ended up trapped inside a public toilet, with a robotic goose and three hoverdrones." Hedy computer-sighed. "Initiating flowchart."

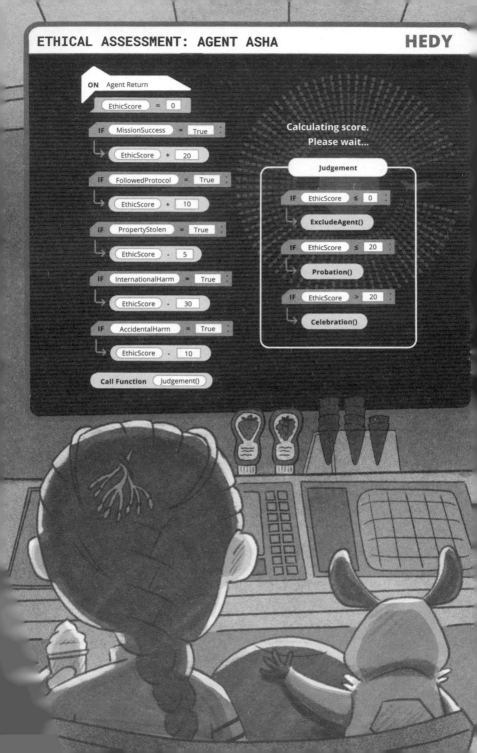

"Nice algorithm," said Asha.

Hedy concluded her analysis and announced: "You achieved your objective and showed initiative, courage and skill."

"It wasn't just me, you should have seen Tyler and Tumble—" Asha began.

Hedy wasn't finished. "You were also reckless, disruptive, disobeyed several orders, were nearly captured on multiple occasions, stole a boat and have just eaten all our emergency supply of raspberry ripple."

There was a pause. Asha tried not to twitch. "However, your actions have been determined as ... more or less justified."

"YES! Thanks, Hedy!" Asha leapt up, sending a splodge of cookie dough flying.

"But there are consequences," said Hedy. "We have decided to lower your status from Agent to Probationary Agent."

Asha froze. "What?"

"This status will be reviewed after your next mission. Congratulations, Probationary Agent Asha."

"Um … what does probationary mean?" asked Asha, pretty sure it wasn't something good, but just at that moment Hedy's screen went black.

A second later another one came to life. It showed Tyler, still on the beach at Fishmouth, grinning.

"I've just started working with Kim Lau," he said. "Turns out she's an engineer for a cable-laying company. We should have Iceland's connection restored very soon and the Internet back up to full speed here within a few days. We so nearly lost that final cable. Our shark had managed a little nibble before we turned up."

"Cool," said Asha distractedly. It was cool, and of course Asha was delighted they had saved the Internet, but she had a more pressing question. "Tyler, do you know what probationary means? Is it bad?"

Tyler's grin faded a little. "You're on probation? No, it's not bad … but it just means Hedy's going to keep an eye on you before making you a full agent. Don't worry! It happens to a lot of first timers."

"Did it happen to you?" demanded Asha.

"No," Tyler admitted. Then he added, "Don't sweat it. All you've got to do is ace your next mission."

"That's all? Saving the Internet isn't enough? That's ridic––" Before Asha could continue, Tyler looked up and to the left, at another window on his screen. He frowned.

"Whoa, got to shoot," he said. "There's a new mission. Rare dolphins have been disappearing from protected areas around the American coast. Also there's a crab in my flipper..." With that, Tyler's screen also went black.

Asha slumped back on her seat, knocking over an empty sprinkles tub. She was a probationary agent? Just because she'd disobeyed one protocol! And stolen one boat! And tried to steal one entire database instead of a single file and been caught in the process. And lied to her parents...

OK. Maybe Hedy did have a point.

Still. A probationary agent was 100 per cent more agent than she had been that morning. At least she was part of the CSA.

But what was the CSA? Who was in charge of it? And who was Hedy? How could an AI be in charge of a global organization? Someone had to have programmed Hedy in the first place.

Just thinking about it made her fingers twitchy. She wanted to write down her thoughts, search online, and call Demola, all at once. But most of all, she couldn't wait to go on another mission.

* * *

The van was swinging onto the road that led to her home. Ice cream was nice, but what she really needed was a bowl of hot dhal. And maybe one of Mum's big bear hugs. And Dad's too. She'd tell them that she wasn't going to sleep over at Demola's because she'd finished her project and wanted to do some maintenance on Drone instead. And then tomorrow, she would do her homework and help make some jalebis.

This weekend, anyway.

Epilogue

April 15 - 16:41

Asha was half-listening to a news stream as she made the final touches to Drone's new panelling. She was hoping to find out what had happened to the robot shark. Had Hedy managed to expose Shelly as the CSA had planned?

"There have been no further reports of shark attacks in the last twelve hours," said the news reader. "Since this morning engineers across the globe have been working non-stop to repair damaged cables. We've just had confirmation that all the original cables are now once again operational. Flights and hospitals can resume a normal service and the global stock market is showing signs of recovery. Shelly Inc has released a statement saying that, in light of these developments, it will suspend its roll-out of ShellyNet for the foreseeable future. Politicians from all sides, however, have praised Shelly Belly for standing with the government in a time of crisis. She is being presented with the National Award for Bravery, for offering her services when the country was on the brink of cyber-disaster. We now go live to the ceremony at Buckingham Palace."

"Euch, what?! That's a total lie!" Asha muttered to Drone, whose eyes flashed a sympathetic green. "Shelly Belly is NOT the hero everyone thinks she is. She's not who I thought she was either."

Asha hadn't told anyone what had happened. Not her parents, not Anushka or even Demola. They had no idea that Asha had broken into Shelly Inc, hidden in a helicopter and won a coding battle on a stolen boat while a robotic shark was trying to eat her.

Her CSA Handbook said she was allowed to tell one person about her agent status, and she knew she could trust Demola. But she wanted to tell him in person. For one thing it was more spy – and she also couldn't wait to see the look on his face. Asha had also decided to tell Nani-Ji, her grandma. Nani-Ji was 1,000 years old and could keep secrets better than anyone Asha knew. And if the CSA found out Asha had told her, they probably wouldn't care anyway. What difference if a little old lady knew?

Asha looked at her tablet screen, where the news stream was still playing. "A rare tiger cub has been kidnapped from Park Zoo." There was a clip of a tiger pacing around her enclosure.

"There are only around three hundred Sumatran

tigers left in the wild," said the reporter. "The zoo's breeding programme brought hope for their survival. But now..."

"Who'd steal a tiger cub?" Asha frowned. "Hey, do you remember what Tyler said about those dolphins going missing? I wonder if..."

Her satellite phone rang. Asha grabbed it from her desk and read the screen.

URGENT INCOMING CALL FROM HEDY

ASHA JOSHI
Status: Sleeping

TIME SPENT SLEEPING:

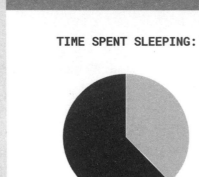

10 hours 12 minutes

LOCATION

Wembley, UK

TIME SINCE LAST USED THE TOILET:
Number 1: 1 hour 37 mins
Number 2: 2 hours 56 mins

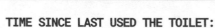

Height gain since yesterday: 0.015cm
Height : 140cm

BATTERY DATA:
Battery data corrupted by shark attack. Please input manually at
www.thisisnota.site

TOTAL DISTANCE TRAVELLED

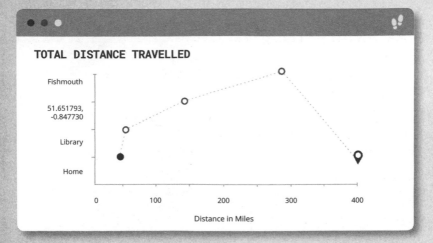

Fishmouth

51.651793,
-0.847730

Library

Home

0   100   200   300   400

Distance in Miles

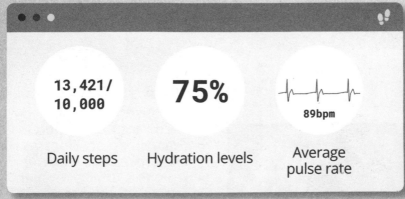

**13,421/
10,000**

75%

89bpm

Daily steps   Hydration levels   Average
pulse rate

SCREEN TIME

2 hours
30 minutes

FACE TO FACE INTERACTION

5 hours
36 minutes

10:06 ACTIVITY LOG 002
Scanning for bots. Suspicious account detected: @Sophie_Deen_ASC.

10:07 INTEL 003
48 million Twitter accounts are bots. 66% of tweets are created by bots, not humans. Twitter is unreliable.

10:50 INTEL 007
A former luxury shopping mall is the HQ for Venezuela's intelligence agency. Spies can be anywhere. Even libraries.

10:55 INTEL 008
Note: Hedy Lamarr was a Hollywood actress and an inventor. In 1942, she invented the 'Secret Communication System' that WiFi is based on.

10:55 INTEL 009
Scientists have invented hardware for computers that can detect illnesses like cancer and diabetes from the smell of human breath. Note: discourage installation. Do not want to smell Asha's breath.

10:58 INTEL 010
Hacking groups are often given animal code names: Sneaky Panda, Golden Rat, Grim Spider.

10:59 WARNING 007

Humans often use the Mercator map. It makes North America look bigger and Africa look smaller than they really are.

The Gall-Peters map is 24% more accurate in terms of land mass. Humans should think more about their map projections, or use globes.

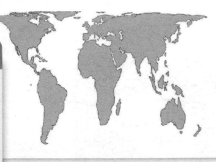

10:59 INTEL 013

Cable companies have reported shark attacks since 1987. Sharks love fibre-optic cables the best. Google now uses Kevlar (a material used in bulletproof vests and invented by Stephanie Kwolek) to keep sharks away.

10:59 INTEL 012

99% of data crossing oceans is transmitted by underwater cables. They connect mainland UK at 52 locations. NOTE: Iceland is connected to the Internet by 4 underwater cables.

10:59 INTEL 014

100% of Iceland's homes have access to the Internet (No.1 in the world!) COMPARISON: In 2018, over 90% of UK homes had Internet access, 88% in the USA, 78% in Europe, 30% across Africa, 7% in Madagascar and 1% in Eritrea. CONSIDER: What impact does this have on the bias and quality of information found online?

NOTE: write pamphlet to explain net neutrality to humans.

11:13 INTEL 015

In 2010 the Stuxnet virus infected an Iranian nuclear facility. The virus was delivered on a memory stick.

11:00 ACTIVITY LOG 004

Surveillance capitalist identified: Shelly Belly.

11:16 INTEL 016

In the 1950s, Central Intelligence Agency agents used a book written by a magician: *The Official CIA Manual of Trickery and Deception.*

11:17 INTEL 017

In 2015, a swimmer was saved by her selfie stick. She was about to be dragged underwater by a deadly current, but someone grabbed her selfie stick and pulled her to safety.

11:22 INTEL 020
On average, Brits check their phones 70 times a day.

11:26 INTEL 024
During WW2, a Dutch ship evaded capture by disguising itself as an island.

In the UK, it's only legal to secretly record someone if you don't share the recording with anyone.
Pretending to be somebody else on the phone is also illegal... If a robot commits a crime, who is punished? The robot, or the person who programmed the robot? UNKNOWN

11:28 INTEL 027
In parts of Nigeria, it's disrespectful to call someone by their name. Other terms, like "Auntie," should be used instead.

11:26 INTEL 023
Morse code was used by secret agents during the Cold War. Radios still receive random bursts of mysterious Morse code today , known as numbers stations.

.... . .-.. .-.. ---

11
Some systems contain a "nuke" password which destroys all data.
ENQUIRY: Do I have a "nuke" password?
Paranoia levels increasing.

12:25 INTEL 028
Shelly Inc HQ is similar to Facebook HQ (garden is the size of 4.5 football pitches) and Apple HQ (walls are made of glass and people keep injuring themselves by walking into them). LOL humans.

12:27 INTEL 029

Facewatch scans faces on CCTV. If face is unknown, then an alarm is activated. NOTE: Drones do not have "faces". Are we detectable?

12:27 INTEL 030

Retinal scanners look at the blood vessels in people's eyes. They are unique, like fingerprints, and can be used to identify humans.

12:27 INTEL 031

Amazon's face-recognition software confused 28 American politicians with criminals. The chance of being mistaken for a criminal was increased if the person scanned was not white. Lack of diversity = ignorance = bad algorithms = bad outcomes.

12:49 INTEL 033

In 2011, the bomb detection scanner at LAX in California was activated when a passenger tried to bring 240 live fish, all packed in watertight suitcases, onto the plane. Humans, ROFL.

13:05 INTEL 036

Bluetooth doesn't interrupt other radio signals on the same wavelength.

13:06 INTEL 037

Shelly Inc discourages employees from going home. NOTE: Apple and Facebook provide sleeping pods for their staff. Is this healthy?

16:10 INTEL 040

The Shortfin Mako is the fastest shark in the world (top speed 46mph).

16:12 INTEL 041

There are roughly 440 species of shark. 100 million sharks are killed each year through hunting and fishing.

16:12 INTEL 042

"Chum" = blood, guts and fish bones. Great white sharks can smell one drop of blood in 10 billion drops of water.

16:15 WARNING 008

Remind humans to use different passwords on different websites ELSE if a hacker gets your password for one site, they can use it for another.

16:12 INTEL 043

In 2018 Vanessa Pirotta created a waterproof drone to collect whale snot. Gross.

16:19 INTEL 044

Australian scientists have trained sharks to tell the difference between jazz and classical music.

16:27 INTEL 044

Other animals affected by Internet cables: birds, mammals, insects. Electromagnetic radiation can confuse an animal's navigation system.

16:36 INTEL 045

Bluetooth travels between 1-100 metres. New devices can extend the distance to over 200 metres.

16:34 WARNING 009

Significant damage to outer casing. Motherboard exposed. Processor exposed. RAM exposed. Avoid liquids. Seek repair immediately.

17:22 ACTIVITY LOG 012

Sleep mode activated. Running dream sequence.

CSA BRIEFING:
MISSION SHARK BYTES

Mission: Save the free Internet from global shutdown

Urgency level: High ⚠️
Deadline: 48 hours

Background:

Sudden loss of Internet.

Unconfirmed reports that it is related
to underwater cable damage in the UK.

Reports of large sharks sighted
near cable locations.

Strong likelihood that Shelly Belly is
connected to the case.

Specialist skills needed:
★ ★ ★
Infiltration, hacking,
marine biology

Mission details:

Agent 1:

Sneak inside Shelly Inc HQ to retrieve
target file located on main server.

Agent 2:

Use intel from target file to
uncover Shelly Belly master plan;
fix the problem.

TOP SECRET

<Missions>   <Case file>   <Suspect file>   <The Internet>   <Top secret>

CSA BRIEFING:
MISSION SHARK BYTES

Other requirements:

Find or recruit an agent in London, UK who could be briefed and travel to the location within 24 hours. Agent must not be known to Shelly Belly's database.

Mission equipment:

- </> Megafart Selfie Stick
- </> What-A-Bottle
- </> Satellite phone
- </> Standard CSA stealth suit
- </> CSA wetsuit
- </> Waterproof notebook
- </> Emergency whistle

- </> Snorkel
- </> Crisps

Mission transport
Ice-cream van

Mission risks and precautions:

⚠ Capture by Shelly Inc

⚠ Indoctrination into Shelly Belly cult of personality

⚠ Appearance in Shelly Belly's social media

⚠ Shark attacks

⚠ Boating accidents

⚠ Missing dinner

DANGER ALERT

CASE FILE:
ASHA JOSHI

Age: 11 years old

Eye colour: Brown

Skills: Coding. Inventing. Asking "why".

Recorded data:

Location:
Wembley

2

**Agility
level**

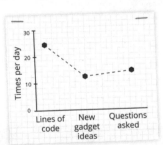

Achievements:

Date	Location	Description
20.05	School	Solar panels installed on the roof of her school
25.05	Home	Upgraded home cybersecurity after teacher's email account was hacked
13.11	School	Climbed the drainpipe to headteacher's third-floor office and hacked her computer
19.12	School	Broke into locker and hid inside in order to miss assembly

<Case file> <Suspect file> <The Internet> <Top Secret> <Missions>

CASE FILE:
ASHA JOSHI

Family tree:

GREAT-GRANDPARENTS

Lahore, Punjab, Pakistan (formerly India)

Surat, Gujarat, India

PARNANA:
Sundershan Suri
Lahore, India

⚭

PARNANI:
Kavita Suri
née Kapoor
Lahore, India

PARDADA:
Krishan Joshi
Surat, India

⚭

PARDADI:
Jyoti Joshi
née Patel
Surat, India

GRANDPARENTS

NANI:
Meera Sahni
née Suri
Nairobi, Kenya

⚭

NANA:
Sachin Sahni
Nairobi, Kenya

DADA:
Anil Joshi
Surat, Gujarat

⚭

DADI/BA:
Sunita Joshi
née Bhasin
Surat, Gujarat

MUMMY:
Priya Joshi
née Sahni
Wembley, UK

⚭

DADDY:
Nikhil Joshi
Wembley, UK

SISTER:
Anushka Joshi
Wembley, UK

Asha Joshi
Wembley, UK

SUSPECT:
SHELLY BELLY

Name: Shelly Belly

Age: 17

FaceSpace followers: 107.8 million

Current Location: London, UK

Recorded data:

Social media celebrity and tech entrepreneur Shelly Belly is the richest and arguably the most popular person on the planet. However, the CSA is tracking Shelly Belly's behaviour after detecting a series of unethical activities:

Brainwashing people with subliminal advertising

Pouring sewage into the ocean

Poo | Water bottles | Crisps | Snot

25% Backwash | 75% Orange juice

Drinking orange juice straight from the carton

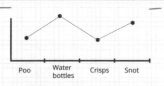

@realshellyb Today at 10.25 AM

Like, share, comment your name and location and follow for a chance to win Shelly Inc shirt! #RealLove

Selling the personal data of her customers

SUSPECT:
SHELLY BELLY

CHILDREN'S SPY AGENCY · QUESTION EVERYTHING

AMANDA

SHELLY INC HQ

Chattr

 @realshellyb Today at 9.19 AM
Woke up to news of further loss of Internet worldwide. I'm so devastated. If you can read this, don't worry, my team and I are working on a solution</3#YouButBetter
Shared by 14k people   ♥ 20.3k

@realshellyb Yesterday at 4.13 PM
Great meeting with @RicardoKonCarney just now while working my glutes on the elliptical #fitnessfriday. Expect some exciting developments from Shelly Inc soon!
Shared by 576k people   ♥ 6.8k

@realshellyb Yesterday at 10.34 AM
It's a beautiful morning at Shelly HQ. My lovely team of dedicated employees are joking around as always. Look at this clown, lying on her face! I love my staff.

shellyinc.life
Shared by 38k people   ♥ 58.2k

Shelly Inc T&Cs

By agreeing to these terms and conditions, you grant Shelly Inc "we", "us", "your bestie" full ownership of all the data on your phone including but not limited to your biometric data, face shape, eye colour and freckle constellation. We may sell your data to politicians, lobbyists and advertisers but don't worry, it's to help improve your user experience.

AGREE

CASE BRIEFING:
THE INTERNET

What is the Internet?

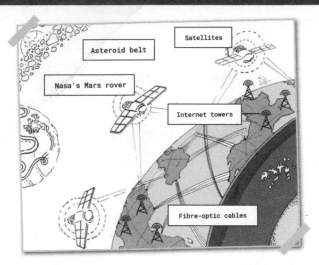

The Internet is a network of computers connected to each other around the world by cables.

We use this global network to share information and talk to each other.

Is the Internet in the sky?

No. Well, sort of. The Internet = computers + cables. Some of the cables are on land and some of them are under the sea. None of them are in a real cloud. ALTHOUGH the Internet can also travel through space via satellites if you live in a remote area or in a really (really) tall tree.

CSA BRIEFING: THE INTERNET

Is the Internet everywhere?

No. Around 49% of the world had access in 2020.

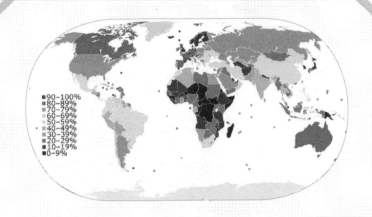

Who wrote the Internet?

Good question. The 49% of people who have access to it, probably.

Who uses it?

Humans and a rare species of otter found in Falso, Yoormum.

<The Internet>   <Suspect file>   <Case file>   <Top secret>

CASE BRIEFING:
THE INTERNET

How does it work?

It's not that complicated:

1. Every computer has an address.

2. Everything on the Internet – emails, websites, files, movies – is made up of data.

3. This data can be sent and received by different computers. It knows where to go because of the computer's address.

4. The data travels through lots of cables to get to its destination.

5. Some of the cables go under the sea. Some of them go over the land.

6. And if the cables break, people can't send or receive things. The Internet breaks.

7. CHAOS AND DRAMA.

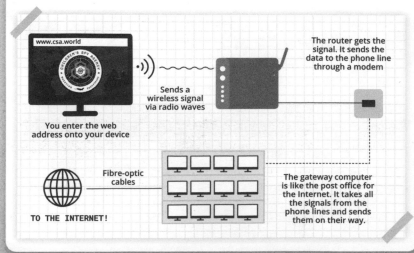

www.csa.world

You enter the web address onto your device

Sends a wireless signal via radio waves

The router gets the signal. It sends the data to the phone line through a modem

Fibre-optic cables

TO THE INTERNET!

The gateway computer is like the post office for the Internet. It takes all the signals from the phone lines and sends them on their way.

<The Internet>   <Suspect file>   <Case file>   <Top secret>   <Missions>

CSA BRIEFING:
THE INTERNET

Can I see it?

You can't see the Internet, the same way you can't see happiness or farts. You can see the effect of it, and how it is made, but you can't see the actual thing.

Is it magic? ★ No.

Do emails really go under the sea?

Yes, if they are being sent to another country. They travel along submarine cables, under the sea.

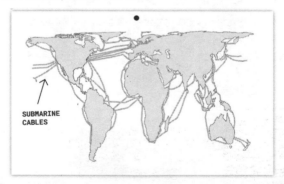

SUBMARINE
CABLES

What happens if the cables break?

If the cables that connect countries to each other break, it's a problem. Whole countries could be cut off from the Internet. We would not be able to send agents the same intel for missions. Other bad things would happen. It would be very dangerous.

WELL DONE.
IF YOU CAN READ THIS YOU'VE
ALREADY PASSED YOUR FIRST TEST.
GO TO WWW.CSA .WORLD/MIRROR
TO START YOUR AGENT TRAINING
OR SCAN THIS QR CODE.

CHILDREN'S SPY AGENCY

QUESTION EVERYTHING

JOIN US
www.csa.world